WILLIAM A. MAYS

The Plot To Assassinate Barack Obama

The Police Gazette
Publishing House

The Police Gazette Publishing House
PO Box 372
Binghamton, NY 13902

www.PoliceGazette.US

The Police Gazette Publishing House is a division of National Police Gazette Enterprises, LLC.
The name and logo for The Police Gazette Publishing House are trademarks of National Police Gazette Enterprises, LLC.

ISBN-10: 0-985-34750-3
ISBN-13: 978-0-9853475-0-5

The Plot To Assassinate Barack Obama

Prologue

What could be more American than making lots of money while protecting families and businesses against the sudden, unexpected death of a key member? Medical doctors may be better at saving actual lives. But you could be financially ruined by the time they're done. Everything you worked and saved for gone.

America is not a place for losing everything to medical bills; it's a place for discovering financial opportunity. Ask the hundreds of thousands of immigrants clamoring to come here every year. America is a place to provide for families and build fortunes. And one of the most basic ways to do that is through life insurance.

Problem is life insurance, vital as it may be to a family's or business's financial security, is almost never top of mind in one's financial planning. It takes an outsider, the life insurance agent or professional, to plant the seed and get people to act in their own best interest. People on their own don't decide one day to get in their car, drive down to the insurance store, and pick up some life insurance. The life insurance salesman has to be proactive. He has to go seek out potential clients and employ the skill of persuasive selling—convincing a person to buy something they hadn't thought they wanted or needed. But if he's done his job right, the life insurance professional has convinced his prospects not that he's selling products; he's really selling hopes and dreams.

Ultimately, though, the work can be very grueling. And all insurance salespeople have a natural hunger for approval and recognition. Fortunately for this dogged group of individuals, there is a nirvana of approval, a Valhalla of recognition. And its name is the Million Dollar Round Table. Every single person who gets into the life insurance business has one goal: to qualify for membership in MDRT.

MDRT is the Mount Olympus of the life insurance and financial services industry. It is the most public recognition of superior achievement in the field of life insurance sales in the world. Qualifying for membership in MDRT is like when Charlie won the chocolate factory. It's as if the hand of Ben Feldman—the greatest life insurance salesman who ever lived—reaches down from heaven and pulls you up and out of the simmering rabble to give you literally a place at The Table.

I really can't think of any other business I'd rather be in.

My name is Hank Stafford, and I provide life insurance.

1

"John Dean is dead."

"Umm, what?" I said, the dreamy sleep still clinging to my mind.

"You said that's how it would start again."

"Yeah, um, okay," I said, there being a lag between the words as I heard them coming through the phone and my full comprehension of their meaning.

"He was the rat, you said. He would be the signal that it's starting again. You know, he would be the 'Luca Brasi sleeps with the fishes' moment."

"Yeah, the rat. What time is it?"

"Three A.M."

"Okay, Hillary," I said. "What can I do for you?"

"You don't remember? You're the one who told me: John Dean was the rat in the Nixon administration. He's the one who spilled the beans to Congress about everything he knew. You said that if John Dean died other than by natural causes it would mark the return to the old approach and it would be a warning to anyone who might be involved."

I sat up.

"Why did you call me Hillary?"

"Wait a minute," I said. "That was all just a mental exercise; you know, a parlor game. I wasn't being serious."

"Well, it made sense to me. And now John Dean is dead."

I paused. Conspiracy theories and hypothetical noodlings were hobbies of mine—as well as of lots of other people. But 99 times out of 100 those hypotheses never came to anything. All just fanciful fictions... 99 times out of 100.

"What did he die of?"

My friend, whose real name was Julia, didn't know what had caused Dean's death. So I got out of bed and started up the computer. Julia suffered from insomnia and had seen the story on CNN. Not wanting to depend on the vagaries of the television news cycle, I got online where my demand for instant gratification could be met at a broadband rate. I read the *New York Times* story on Dean:

> John W. Dean III, former counsel to President Richard Nixon and a figure in the Watergate scandal of the 1970s, was found dead yesterday in the driveway of his home in Beverly Hills, California.
>
> A Beverly Hills police official, speaking on condition of anonymity due to the ongoing nature of the investigation, said that Mr. Dean had been found at approximately 5:30 p.m. by a landscaper employed by the Deans. No cause of death was given.

No cause of death yet. Okay, at that point it could have been anything—a heart attack, a stroke, spontaneous human combustion, anything. Of course I couldn't get back to sleep, because Julia had reawakened The Theory. It hadn't entered my mind for years. But like a down-and-out-relative who comes for a visit and then stays longer than you expect—or hope—once reintroduced to my mind, The Theory began to make itself at home again.

The details of it churned and replayed in my head. At the base was the question: why had there been so many assassinations and attempted assassinations in the 1960s, 70s, and into the 80s? During one 18-year period—1963 to 1981—our nation experienced an acute outbreak of assassinationitis. Presidents, presidential candidates, and cultural leaders were dropping like flies.

Ten serious attempts were made against prominent people during this period, averaging more than one every two years. Six of these were successful, ending the lives of John F. Kennedy, Malcolm X, Martin Luther King, Jr., Robert Kennedy, Harvey Milk, and John Lennon—JFK's alleged assassin Lee Harvey Oswald was also knocked off for good measure. George Wallace and Ronald Reagan were injured, but survived, while Gerald Ford escaped an assassin's bullet not once, but twice. No other 18-year period in American history comes close to this record.

The Theory held that lone nuts could not have accounted for all of this tumult. The number of lone nuts as a percentage of the population should remain fairly constant through time. And in fact, only one assailant who went to trial—John W. Hinckley, Jr., the man who shot Reagan—was determined to have been insane.

So what other variables could account for such a spike during this period? Could assassination have been employed by parties unknown as a political tool? Character assassination has long been a feature of the struggle for political power in this country. And that continues to this day. But for a time, it seems, corporal assassination was added into the mix. Just another device to be used for achieving goals.

But assassination as a tool employed by powerful interests began to wane with the congressional and presidential investigations of the mid to late 1970s. Other methods took over. Even so—considering what had been going on—the mere thought that one could be the target of a plot was enough to keep in line those who would undertake a bid for the highest office. Bill Clinton had mentioned in passing once that he would try for more radical change, but didn't "want to get shot in the head."

Those investigations of the 1970s began with the big bang of the Watergate Hearings, hearings that exposed not assassination, but a wide array of less-lethal dirty tricks employed by those working for Richard Nixon. Those folks were minor-league versions of their more deadly counterparts, employing mostly burglary, bugging, and forgery to accomplish goals against enemies. But those dirty tricks became the most well-known examples in the public mind of how some with political power in this country will stoop to stunning illegalities in order to maintain control of the most powerful nation on earth. The word "Watergate" has been seared into the American conscious as a result.

Any illegal plot, big or small, has one rule that needs to be followed if the subterfuge is to remain undetected: keep your mouth shut, and if forced to open it, lie. The more serious the illegality, the more serious the consequence for those who break this rule. The first person in a high position within the Nixon administration to come forward and spill all the beans he knew to the congressional committee was John Dean. He was a load-bearing wall in the house of cards that then came tumbling down. If an Age of Assassination were ever to return, I theorized, John Dean would be the first one dispatched as he's the most publicly well known snitch in the field of destroying political enemies. It would be a clear message that those with heavier hands were back in business.

But as I told Julia, The Theory was simply a mental exercise. If I were 100% sure that that's what was going on, I would probably have been a member of some underground resistance organization instead of selling life insurance for the National American Life Insurance Company of Maryland.

I thought it was clear something funny was going on with some of those killings back then, that there was more there than met the eye. But did I have concrete evidence proving what exactly had happened and who was involved? No. An oil tanker full of circumstantial evidence, but no direct, undeniable links that led to something other than the official conclusions—themselves based mainly on shaky and circumstantial evidence. The lawyers in the first O.J. trial would have had a field day with that stuff. But in any case, there was nothing solid upon which I could hang my hat.

So I went on with my life. One does not take a break from life-insurance sales. It's a commissions game. The shark needs to keep swimming or the business dries up. If you're not making sales you're not making income. And since the vast majority of new business comes from referrals, you've got to be out there seeing people.

We see and discuss personal financial issues with every type of person from every walk of life. President John F. Kennedy himself once said, "Surely Americans derive their image of business most often from the relations which they establish with insurance agents. The varied services performed by American insurance can do much to carry forward our traditions of freedom." Amen to that, brother.

So I got back out there, and let the long-lost relative who'd come to visit my mind have his own room in exchange for a promise to refrain from disturbing me too often. That was the deal, at least, until I met Amber Manderville.

2

When I say this business runs on referrals, usually what happened was I got a name from a client and then I gave them a call. Life insurance and long-term investments—though everyone says are important—are not the kinds of things that people tend to take the initiative in obtaining. If they do, they tend to be people who are well into middle age and have started to develop health problems. Mortality suddenly starts to become a possibility and that's when they start thinking life insurance.

But Amber was different. First of all, she contacted me, having gotten my name from one of my clients in DC. Second, she came to see me at my office in Beltsville. Usually, it's the agent who makes a house or business call. And third, she was young and quite healthy.

I noticed the third as soon as she walked in the door, my corresponding thoughts being guilt free as I was a divorcee of two years and currently single. But the conversation quickly turned to business. If a romantic play were ever to be considered on a prospective client, it would—at the very least—have to wait until after they signed on the dotted line and became an actual client.

We went to a conference room and sat at the big table. She

smelled great. Perfume, but not too much. Tall, but not taller than me. Dressed nice. I gave her my usual purpose-process-payoff spiel. "The purpose of our meeting today is for me to understand where you are financially and where you'd like to be, and for you to get to know me and National American Life Insurance of Maryland. The process will be for me to describe a little about myself and the financial strength of National American Life. Then I'll ask you some questions that will help me determine what your financial needs, hopes and dreams are. The payoff is I'll be able to come back to you with a package that will help you to reach your goals."

I got out my standard fact-finder questionnaire, which explored a wide range of details in the lives of the prospective client and her family, and found out she was married—a fact that put a damper if not the full kybosh on any potential post-curricular activities. Not to mention, in order for the sales pitch to have maximum effect both Amber and her husband should have been together in front of me. More often than not, if you give the pitch to one spouse without the other, the one who wasn't there will kill the idea as soon as they're informed of it. Spouses do not make good surrogate salespeople. Still, I gave her the full treatment. She came to me, after all; I didn't have to travel. And I would feel like a traitor to my sex if I didn't give this fine-looking woman my full attention.

She and her husband had no children and were expecting none. They rented half of a duplex in Wheaton, Maryland, where Amber worked as an elementary school teacher. Then she told me about her husband. Todd Manderville was in the military. To be specific, he was in the Army, a corporal in the 3rd U.S. Infantry to be more specific.

I went on to ask the usual set of questions about financial concerns. But there was something about Amber's replies that struck me as a little bit off.

"At what age would you like to have the financial ability to retire?" I asked.

"Oh, I'm expecting to be able to retire pretty soon," she said.

"In today's dollars, what monthly income would make you comfortable in retirement?"

"In today's dollars? That's what it's going to be."

"Are you satisfied with the amount of money you have been able to accumulate to this point?"

"No, but that should change soon."

"When investing, how much of a risk taker are you?"

"Oh, I don't like to take risks. But my husband does."

"How concerned are you about you or your spouse maintaining your standard of living in case one of you dies?"

"He doesn't have to worry about me dying. But it's possible he won't be around much longer."

And it went on like that. The questions actually were not so much for my information as they were a way to get the prospective client to focus on her urgent family financial issues. In other words, it's all part of the sales game. I could have asked follow-up questions and explored further what Amber meant by comments that, to some, could seem like red flags. But for the present, I let sleeping dogs lie—like a defense lawyer who doesn't want his client to say anything the lawyer doesn't want to hear. Typically, this approach might involve a business client who happened to make a considerable amount of his income off the books and who desired to find a place to put all that cash where it wouldn't be sitting around in bank accounts—into life insurance policies (which are largely tax-exempt), annuities, and mutual funds, for example. The less I knew in that case, the better. Besides, National American had a very good underwriting department whose job it was to keep agents from getting cases paid—or rather, to ask the tough questions and make sure the company is not taking on too much risk.

Being in the military, of course, is an instant risk, but that did not automatically preclude someone from obtaining life insurance from NALIC of Maryland. The company considered rank, branch of service, whether the country was at peace or war, the person's duty, and there were geographic restrictions. Then, of course, the policy holder had to pay through the nose.

The next step in the process with Amber was to add up "survivor needs" for both spouses. These were amounts that should be set aside for things like funeral expenses, a rent fund, debt liquidation, income maintenance, miscellaneous emergency funds, etc. If there are children involved it goes considerably higher. But in Amber and Todd's case, I didn't figure they'd need more than around $800,000 of life insurance coverage for Todd and $500,000 for Amber, tops.

I went over with her the choices of products she and Todd could use to make up that gap. I explained the basic differences between "term" and "permanent" life insurance. I preferred selling permanent—and not just because the commissions are higher. It's actually better for the client in a number of ways. Permanent insurance—generally whole life or universal life—doesn't expire and as a rule has premiums that never go up. Even better, the policy accumulates a cash value that the policy holder may dip into while the insured is still living. So you've got the best of both worlds: a death benefit to be paid to a beneficiary when you die and an investment with guarantees to grow higher over the years that you can choose to cash in whenever you like.

Term life insurance is best used for temporary life insurance needs, anything from parents wishing to cover themselves until their children are grown and on their own to businesses insuring key employees in the event that one dies and leaves the company vulnerable to loss as a result. Term has no cash value and, though its premium starts out cheaper than permanent insurance, the premium rises with the age of the covered individual. The only way it provides a financial benefit is if the covered person dies sooner than their normal life expectancy.

When I began pushing the benefits of permanent insurance Amber stopped me short. That's when she started to say the things that I didn't want to hear, followed by something that clicked in a very big way.

"I don't think Todd is going to live very much longer."

I think I visibly cringed. "Oh really?" I said. "Is he in Iraq or Afghanistan?"

"No, he's based at Fort Myer in Arlington."

"Arlington... Virginia?"

"Yes."

"What does he do there?"

"He's a sentinel at the Tomb of the Unknowns."

"The Tomb of the Unknown Soldier? At Arlington National Cemetery?"

"Yes." Amber had a calm, matter-of-fact—though vaguely melancholy—delivery. She seemed a little too resigned for someone who believed her husband was about to die.

"Is that normally a dangerous assignment?"

"No, it's probably the safest place he could be in the whole military."

"Then, I'm not quite sure I understand your concern. Does he have a medical condition?"

"No. It's because of something he told me the other day."

She went on to describe something that happened between her and Todd, something she didn't understand, but that convinced her Todd more than likely would not be alive three months from this day.

"He was in the garage," she said. "When he's out there I usually just leave him alone. He's got his tools and stuff out there and that's where he goes for his alone time. But a few days ago, I got one of those feelings that something wasn't right. So I went out to check on him and when I got there he was studying something in a notebook. He was concentrating very hard and I guess he didn't hear me come in. I walked up behind him and looked over his shoulder. I read some of the stuff in the notebook and I couldn't tell what it was. It didn't make any sense. So I read something out loud. Now usually what happens when I sneak up on him is he gets startled and jumps. He hates it when I do that. But he didn't jump this time."

"What did you read in the notebook?" I asked.

"Like I say, none of it made any sense, but I saw somebody's name. It said 'Please pay to the order of Artemus Schreckengost.'"

"That's what you said to him?"

"Yeah, and I asked him who's Artemus Schreckengost. That's when he turned around and, like I say, he didn't jump, but he had this look. I mean Todd told me about this thing soldiers get when they're in combat called the 'thousand-yard stare.' Well he looked like he had that."

"What did he say to you?"

"That's when it started to get weird. He looked at me with that stare and the first thing he said was 'You're Amber Manderville, my wife.' I said, 'Yeah, honey, I know.' I asked him what's the matter and that's when he told me everything. And that's why I want to get $10,000,000 of term life insurance on him as soon as I can."

At that point I think I was startled and jumped. I had to explain to her that the higher the amount of coverage the more involved and detail oriented our underwriting department got. And, technically, I would have to tell them that she had told me there's reason to believe his life may be cut short.

"But you don't have to tell them, do you?"

She looked at me wishfully. She was just beautiful enough for me to show hesitation. And that's when she knew she had me. Choosing to somewhat change the subject, I asked her to go into the details of what Todd had told her. It was that decision at that exact moment in my first conversation with Amber Manderville, that changed my life forever.

She said she spent an hour and a half in that garage with Todd; almost the whole time he was in that thousand-yard-stare state and spoke as if he barely knew her. She said Todd told her he was a member of an extremely elite special operations team. The team was under the direction of the 3rd U.S. Infantry, the National Threat Assessment Center of the U.S. Secret Service, and one other entity that Todd did not know by name.

"He said that his superiors have uncovered a plan in the working," Amber said. "They know President Obama is going to be killed soon."

I knew then what a lottery winner feels like when he first looks at his ticket, and there is a space of time between the moment when his eyes see the winning number in his hand and when his mind accepts that vision as reality. I was right. The Theory was right. And not only was The Theory right, I myself had been thrust into the middle of the unfolding events.

Amber said Todd had told her the coming attempt on

President Obama's life was a very highly developed operation by people with a lot of resources, a level of planning and ability for execution that indicated the marriage of an al Qaeda-style organization—though not al Qaeda itself—with some world-class nation's intelligence and military apparatus.

"Yeah, I'll bet," I said.

"Todd said it probably wasn't some country like Iran. He said they thought it was so complex it had to be somebody like Russia, or even Israel or France."

"Some country with the most highly developed intelligence and secret operations capabilities in the world," I said. "Uh huh, yep, I got it."

"He said that's why this can't be handled by the Secret Service or FBI alone. They can't be stopped by just killing or arresting some of the people involved. And Todd says they still don't know who the actual assassin is going to be. That's when they came to Todd and asked him to be part of this team and swear to give his life to protect the president."

"Did you ask him why they chose him?"

"Well, he's in the 3rd U.S. Infantry. When the president needs military protection they're the ones who have that responsibility. Though Todd's in a different company; he's a sentinel at the Tomb. But if you knew him you would know that he would volunteer for anything they asked, and give his life for his duty without another thought."

"I see." I was absolutely giddy inside. I was sure that one area of the government had stumbled upon the assassination preparations of a different, rogue element of the same government. Our government. The only questions were which elements were the good guys and which were the bad, and did the good guys know they were dealing with people who were supposedly playing on the same team. After years of studying and ruminating on the arcane shenanigans of the United States government, I felt like I'd taken a wrong turn and ended up in the room where it was all being planned. But Amber wasn't through with me yet.

"Todd told me it was better than 50-50 that this would be a suicide mission. But it's supposed to be top secret." She paused, knowing exactly what she was doing. "So that's not something you would tell the underwriting department, is it?"

Try as I did to keep my cards close to the vest, they must have been flying out left and right. "All I can say is 'Wow,'" I replied. "I never thought of using national security as an excuse to keep information from the NALIC of Maryland underwriting department before."

"So how much would it be to buy $10,000,000 of term coverage?"

I laughed, probably more a nervous laugh than anything else. "Well first of all, no matter what I say to underwriting, they're going to want a few things if we're talking about that amount of coverage. Even though Todd's under 30 and doesn't smoke, they'll want a complete medical exam including full blood and urine profiles and electrocardiogram. Is that something Todd would be okay with?"

"I think he would do it."

"Okay. They'll also want to interview him. Do you think he's likely to tell them any of that stuff he told you in the garage the other night?"

"I've asked him about it since then and he pretends he doesn't know what I'm talking about. It really is top secret. I don't know why he told me that night. But it might have been to warn me, because he'd want me to be able to take care of myself. So now I'm taking care of myself."

"Did he ever tell you who Artemus Schreckengost was?"

"No, I asked him again at the end of the talk and he didn't answer. But that's when he started to come around and act more normal. He put his stuff away and said we should go inside."

"Okay," I said. "Let's go for $5,000,000 in coverage. The proceeds are tax free; no sense in getting greedy."

3

I'd ended the meeting with Amber Manderville having set up an appointment to see Todd at their home so I could ask him a few basic health, occupation and hobby questions, have him sign the application, and set up an appointment with a physician for his exam. But what I couldn't get out of my mind wasn't the halfway-decent commission I'd be getting if this thing actually went through, it was Todd Manderville's relationship with the U.S. Army's 3rd Infantry, the Secret Service's National Threat Assessment Center, Artemus Schreckengost, the other unnamed entity, and the fact that Amber had inflated the reasonably dormant Theory into a Mount Rushmore in my brain. I couldn't stop thinking about it. There was every reason to believe President Obama was at risk, and I lay awake that night laboriously churning the details.

Barack Obama was elected during a political sea-change in 2008. There were firsts galore and things people hadn't seen happen in generations. He had the youthful good looks and charisma of John F. Kennedy, the brains of Abraham Lincoln, and the can-do spirit of Franklin D. Roosevelt. Coincidentally, or perhaps not, all three of those men had been the targets of assassins. But riding a meteoric rise, seemingly avoiding the usual compromises of the soul one makes in order to get a shot at the top, Barack Obama brought the promise of change and doing things differently. He was decidedly outside the gang of usual suspects for the top office in the land. And, more crucially, he promised to change the approach to the so-called Global War On Terror from a military-intervention-centered policy to a diplomacy-centered policy.

Additionally, for those who preferred the status quo, Barack Obama began to crack the Republican grip on the South for the first time in nearly 50 years. With the exception of Hubert Humphrey winning Texas in 1968, no non-Southern Democrat had won any Southern state since 1960. Barack Obama won Virginia, North Carolina, and nearly won the deep-south Georgia, getting 47% of the vote. Here was a man outside the traditional controlling influences of the Washington corridors of power, who was eating away at the ruling class' long-established bases of support. And who had a popular groundswell at his foundation. His face graced magazine covers and collectible merchandise as if he were a movie star. No president since Kennedy—if not FDR—had created such an emotional connection with the American people. He was disquietingly untethered to the most powerful interests in the United States.

The next morning, after about an hour and a half of sleep, I called my client in DC who'd referred Amber my way. I wanted to get anything she knew about the Mandervilles. Debbie Poindexter was Amber's cousin and worked at OSHA, the Occupational Safety & Health Administration. Debbie had told me previously that she was related to Admiral John Poindexter who had been a national security advisor for Ronald Reagan, an Iran-Contra defendant, and the head of an office under George W. Bush that developed the Policy Analysis Market—a futures-market system designed to predict assassinations, coups d'état, terrorist strikes, and other turbulent political events. She claimed to have never met him and, in this case, I concluded that sometimes coincidences really were just coincidences.

When I spoke to her I thanked her again for the referral. I couldn't divulge any detailed information to her about Amber and Todd—the two reasons being my fiduciary duty to protect my new clients' confidential financial information and my own selfish desire to keep what Amber had told me about Todd's mission to myself. I was privy, apparently, to some very narrowly disseminated secrets and I wasn't about to start blabbing them around and have amateurs stepping on my toes as I pursued my research.

"I don't know how to put this without casting unfair aspersions on Amber and Todd," I told Debbie. "So please don't think that there's something wrong with them. It's just that, in order to maintain the highest quality possible, our underwriting department will choose clients at random for double-special review." When in doubt, blame underwriting. I continued, "So nothing unique with Amber and Todd, just a random review. With that in mind, have you ever seen or heard of Amber or Todd doing anything you would consider unusual or strange?"

Debbie said that she and Amber were friendly as cousins, although not particularly close. From what she could tell, however, there was nothing unusual or strange about Amber and her husband.

"So no psychotic episodes that you know of, or delusions, hallucinations, what have you?"

Debbie assured me that Amber and Todd were as normal as they came. Then she expressed relief that the NALIC of Maryland underwriting department hadn't singled her out for review, and we ended our conversation.

Doing some internet research, I verified a few other tidbits

Amber had told me. The 3rd U.S. Infantry is, indeed, the Army's regiment based in the Washington DC area whose responsibility is to escort the president, provide security for Washington in times of crisis, and perform ceremonial duties like guarding the Tomb of the Unknowns at Arlington National Cemetery. The regiment is known as the "Old Guard" because it's been part of the U.S. Army longer than any other, first appearing in the 18th century.

The National Threat Assessment Center is the research and analysis branch of the Secret Service, itself an agency within the Department of Homeland Security. The NTAC specializes in figuring out what makes a person likely to mount an attack on a public figure. Their research and recommendations are given to the Secret Service and other law enforcement agencies as a way to help prevent such attacks. Not quite "Minority Report" stuff, but going in that direction.

When I researched Artemus Schreckengost I hit a dead end. But my research was done with publicly available records. Maybe this guy wasn't so public. Maybe he was decidedly underground. Maybe he was someone who had yet to come in from the cold, as it were. This name, I decided, could be my ace in the hole, so I resolved to guard it, well, not with my life—I'm not crazy—but certainly closely.

Then there was the unnamed "other entity." Not knowing how to approach this one I decided to go out into the field. If there's one thing I learned in my line of work, it's there's only so much you can do from the office. Eventually you have to get out and do some face to face.

4

I arrived at 950 H Street NW in Washington, the home of the United States Secret Service. Upon entering, a friendly security guard asked what floor I was going to and whom I was there to see. I showed him my business card and said I had an appointment with someone in the National Threat Assessment Center, but I'd forgotten their name. He got on the phone and made a call, telling whoever picked up I was there for my appointment. There was a pause and then the guard told me they had no record of any such appointment. I said I would recognize the person if I saw them, could I please just go up and.... The guard interrupted me saying this was a no go. That's when I guessed I had to pull out my ace.

"Oh, I just remembered! I'm here to see Artemus Schreckengost."

The guard reported this over the phone. There was a brief pause and then the phone disconnected. Calling back, the guard repeated whom I was there to see. There followed a much longer pause. I used the opportunity to ask the guard if they provided a good retirement plan there where he worked. He told me he hadn't given it much thought. When someone came back on the other end of the line, the guard said "Okay" and told me I could go up. He summoned another guard to serve as my escort. I told him to keep my business card and give me a call about retirement plans.

My escort, who didn't say a word the entire time we were together, took me up an elevator. The car stopped at "3" and the door opened onto a blandly colored hallway with no decoration or signage, not even a floor number. A man in his late 30s wearing a nice suit greeted us. The guard returned to the elevator and I was left alone with my new host.

"Welcome to the Secret Service, Mr. Stafford," he said.

"Call me Hank," I replied, putting on my best friendly-yet-confident smile. "And you are?"

"Come with me," was all he said.

We walked to the end of the totally barren hallway. He waved a card in front of a sensor and opened the door. Behind it was a small room, about 12 feet square, equally as drab as the hallway we'd just left. It's total contents were a table and two chairs.

"Now, what can we do for you?" my host said after we sat.

"I'm with National American Life of Maryland." I gave him my card. "I was referred by a very special client of mine who said that one of your employees was interested in exploring financial security."

"And your client's name?"

"You know, that's the funny thing. Normally my clients are not just willing but eager to let the referred person know who did the referring, to let them know whom they can credit for helping to solve their family's money worries. But in this case my client asked to remain anonymous."

"Oh, that's too bad, because I'd really like to know who to thank."

"So you're Mr. Schreckengost?"

My host smiled and said, "No, I'm not Mr. Schreckengost."

"Is Mr. Schreckengost available?"

"I might be able to answer if you could tell me where you got that name."

"You see, I have a fiduciary responsibility to my clients. You may be familiar with what that means. But I like to extend it to keeping confidential anything that they ask me, within reason."

"Then, I'm afraid there's no one who works here by that name."

"Okay, can I ask you a question? Are you with the National Threat Assessment Center?"

"No," was all he said.

"'No' as in I can't ask, or 'no' as in you're not with the National Threat Assessment Center?"

He shrugged and said "Take your pick. My main concern is when a person tries to gain access to a Secret Service facility under false pretense, I'd like to find out why."

I nodded while I thought of a way to go. "I made it up. Artemus Schreckengost. I made the name up. It's because of the managing partner at my general office. He wants to see my numbers come up. I mean he's really putting the pressure on me. He said if I didn't start seeing more quality prospects he was going to ask me to resign from the company. But I can't, because life insurance, care-free retirement, solid investments, and long-term care for our elderly relatives is something I really care about passionately. Mission before commission is what I always say. So, I felt like I had to think of creative ways to get inside and talk to respected professionals like yourself about securing their financial futures with just a few dollars a month. As you can see, it seems to have worked."

"Why would you make up a name like that?"

"I don't know. It sounds important, doesn't it?"

"Important?"

"Yeah. It's got a lot of syllables."

"Why did you decide the NTAC was the place you wanted to gain access?"

"Hey, it's the inner workings of the Secret Service. If I could offer my services to folks in there it could snowball throughout the agency. Word of mouth is very powerful in my line of work. Once people find out how easy it is to get started on a plan that assures college funding for the kids and a happy retirement for themselves, they like to tell their friends."

"You're not going to tell me the truth are you?"

"Sir, I sell life insurance. I completely understand how you feel. Many people I've spoken to have felt the exact the same way as you. But they found after seeing an illustration of not just the current, but guaranteed, cash value you can expect to have in your policy 20 or 30 years from now, that it's not too good to be true; it really is true."

My host paused. I also paused, a well-placed silence in the conversation being as important as any word that can be spoken. Finally, he said, "Okay, thank you, Mr. Stafford. I'll take you back to the lobby."

"So, do you think anyone here might have an interest in hearing about any of the services I can offer?"

"Let's go," was all he said.

Out on the street I went over what had just happened. Was it just a coincidence that they became willing to see me only after I mentioned Artemus Schreckengost? It did seem my host's main concern was where I got the name. But, damn it, there was still nothing concrete. My only consolation was I made two contacts in my life-insurance and financial-services prospecting.

5

I'd never seen before, in person, the changing of the guard at the Tomb of the Unknowns at Arlington National Cemetery. I'd read about it and seen pictures, but until you are right there watching it happen you can't apprehend the full impact of its surreality. The military as a whole is known for training its members in precise movements and drills. But the sentinels of the Tomb perform the most precise and uniform movements in the entire armed services. The indoctrination, conditioning, and commitment of a soldier in this assignment has to be consummate. To say the movements are robotic would be one way to put it, though robots are not usually thought of as being this fluid. A more accurate description might be they display the relentless, i.e., non-human, perfection of computer animation. Someone could do CG of one series of a sentinel's movements, then put it on a loop and it would be an exact match to what goes on at the Tomb 24 hours a day, 365 days a year. The strangeness of it is such that if a sentinel were seen behaving in this manner out in the general public he might be considered psychotic.

Given this, I wondered what Todd would be like when I met him. I'd seen people who were so gung ho and hyper-serious about the United States' mission as the preeminent nation on earth that if they smiled or accepted a joke, it seemed like they'd have to commit hara-kiri. And these sentinel guards appeared to be the most serious among the serious. It was clear whatever mission Todd had been asked to perform, he would do it with the utmost conviction.

But the meeting would have to wait until I arranged some changes with Amber. My little tree-shaking visit to the Secret Service had alerted them to the fact I knew the name Artemus Schreckengost, and they seemed very eager to find out how I came to know that name. I considered it a safe assumption that my actions would no longer be going unnoticed. So I bought a TracFone and called Amber at her school.

I suggested we have the meeting somewhere else, saying I'd forgotten I'd made an appointment with the owner of the bowling alley in White Oak for very soon after the one I had scheduled with them. It was near the Naval Surface Weapons Center, only a 10 or 15 minute drive away. I said we could meet in the snack bar and take care of our business. Amber agreed on one condition, that we actually bowl a couple of games. I said it was duckpins, a more difficult—and to me frankly silly—variation on regular bowling. She said, "I don't care. I just think it would be fun to bowl with you."

The thing about salesmen is we're always looking for any sort of favorable response from those we're soliciting. Duckpins had nothing to do with closing a $5,000,000 policy, unless it was something the client wanted. Then duckpins had everything to do with closing a $5,000,000 policy. The fact that she was personally praising me went over just fine. I'd take praise with a premium check any day.

So I agreed, but I had one condition, that they let me pay for it. Amber was delighted as the date was set. But she made one final request. "I spoke to Todd about the insurance," she said, "and he thinks it's a good idea, but can you help me with something? Don't tell him how much it's for. Don't say it's for $5,000,000. Can you do that for me?"

Amber was asking me to engage in another moral dilemma. Fortunately, the wrong side of any moral dilemma has a rationale that can justify it. And there was something about her that made me open to doing what she asked. I reasoned that since Amber would be the actual owner of the policy, not Todd, it was really up to her how to handle it. Todd just had to go through the underwriting process and sign the application—a signature that would be on a separate page from the page that showed the amount of the policy. And that signature was essentially just to release information and declare that his answers represented his best knowledge. There was no need to show him the amount of the policy unless he got nosey. "Okay," I said, "if he asks let's tell him it's for $500,000."

I figured I could write in that amount without any commas, then add the commas and extra zero later. If Todd saw the amount of the premium it wouldn't make any difference since I wouldn't have shown him the sample illustration as I had Amber. He didn't know how much the premium would be for any particular amount of insurance. "Thank you, Hank," she said. "I'll see you on Wednesday." Amber and I were beginning to keep secrets from her husband, and, to be honest, it felt a little more stimulating than it probably should have.

I drove to White Oak, parked in a lot some distance from the bowling alley, and walked a roundabout route the rest of the way to be sure I wasn't followed. Inside, I saw Amber sitting at a table behind the lanes with a man I assumed to be Todd. There were a good number of people there, including a few Navy types in uniform. Open bowling was going to end soon so the alley could get ready for its Wednesday-night leagues. Amber saw me, stood up, and introduced her husband.

Todd Manderville struck me as a very normal, regular kind of guy. Any assumptions about how he would behave based on my observation of the sentinels at the Tomb were apparently misplaced.

"Yeah, people think that a lot," he told me. "But we have a duty at the Tomb that we take very seriously. When I'm not at my post, I'm as goofy as the next guy. All the other sentinels are the same way."

The amount of mind control to separate those two worlds, I thought, must have been extraordinary.

We got our shoes and balls and went to our lane where I got out the insurance application and set up at the scoring table. My membership in the American Bowling Congress as an officially sanctioned league bowler meant the scoring duties fell to me. It turned out Todd could have used some of the precision he employed at the Tomb to help his bowling game. Neither he nor Amber were very accomplished.

As we bowled our two games I alternated between keeping the scores and completing the NALIC of Maryland life insurance application, giving a twist to the usual bowling-alley banter in the process. Todd rolled a gutter ball and I asked him, "In the last two years, have you been unable to work or unable to attend school or been disabled for one month or more?"

"No," he replied, then got four pins on his second ball.

So the afternoon went:

Todd rolled a 7/10 split. I asked him, "In the last two years, have you been in a hospital or other medical facility for more than five consecutive days?"

He said, "No" and then rolled a field goal.

Todd got his first strike in the 9th frame of the first game. I asked him, "Have you used tobacco or nicotine in any form in the last five years?"

"Yes," he said, "the second-hand smoke was thick like fog in the parking lot."

"That's a 'no,'" I said.

Over the course of his 10th frame—following his only strike in the 9th—his first ball went in the gutter and his second picked up just the 7-pin. I asked him, "In the last two years, have you engaged in or do you now intend to engage in aircraft flying other than as a passenger, motorcycle driving, snowmobile driving, motorized racing, scuba diving, ballooning, parachuting, hang gliding, ultralight flying, mountaineering, rodeo riding...."

Considering the luck he was having on the lanes, while being barraged with strange personal questions, Todd kept his cool and remained friendly throughout. He seemed to have the demeanor of someone who could be trusted with a stressful mission.

Amber herself posed a bit of a distraction. I strained to keep my eyes off of her as she made her approach to the lane, released, and followed through. In her form-fitting leggings, Amber made the picture of curved, extended beauty every time her ball hit the wood. But discretion was particularly needed as her husband was looking directly at me most of the time while we discussed his life insurance application. I soldiered on.

"In the last five years, have you had your driver's license suspended or revoked?"

"Not suspended. I've gotten a few speeding tickets in my time."

"In the last five years, have you been convicted of a crime

or served time in prison because of a conviction, been arrested for any reason?"

"No, but I plan to," he said. Amber and I looked at each other. He continued with a smile, "I'm going shoot the guy who invented duckpins."

"In the last two years, have you traveled or resided outside the U.S. or Canada or do you intend to do so within the next 12 months?"

"In the next 12 months?"

"Yes, within the next 12 months."

"I don't know," he said with a thoughtful, quizzical look on his face, as if the question had jogged something he couldn't quite remember.

"Well, if you don't have any specific plans, that's a 'no.'"

We finished our games. Amber had won the bragging rights in her household, bowling a 48 and an 80, while Todd had bowled a 57 and a 69. I bowled a 103 and a 123, not bad for duckpins. But the important thing was the application was complete and Todd had signed it. We called his doctor's office and set up his exam and Amber wrote me a check for the first month's premium. She looked at me a long time as she handed it over.

I hadn't bothered asking Todd about the coming attempt on President Obama's life. If he wouldn't talk to Amber about it after that night in the garage, why would he talk to me? I did tell him I was fascinated with the "Old Guard" and the sentinels and how all that worked. I asked if he could give me referrals to his fellow soldiers in the 3rd Infantry. He was reluctant at first, but I gave him my usual story about how my business is dependent upon referrals. I said if he'd had a good experience and believed in the coverage, then I would appreciate the names of 10 friends and relatives to whom I could offer similar services. Ten was a lot he said, but he finally decided he could do three.

6

I stopped by the office to make copies and submit the application for processing, then went home. But as I got out of my car and approached my front door, a man dressed in a suit—who seemed to come out of nowhere—walked very briskly right at me wearing a remarkably stern expression. When he got within three feet he raised his right arm straight out and pointed something at my face. It was an ID card. Gruffly he said, "Special Agent Theodore Turdington, FBI."

I froze. He continued in a rapid crescendo, "What's your name? What's your name? What's your name?"

"I'm Hank Stafford."

He got extremely close to me and continued speaking, like a baseball manager arguing with an umpire. If he'd been wearing a cap, he would have had to turn it around. "Do you have any weapons on you? Tell the truth. I could frisk you right now."

"You could?" I said, thinking I'd heard of some minor statute called the 4th Amendment. "No, I don't have any weapons."

"What about drugs? Do you smoke the weed? Do ecstasy?"

"No, why are you asking me these questions? What's going

on?"

He shouted so loud I thought my eardrum would split. "I'm investigating a very serious matter that involves the national security of the United States of America! The FBI National Security Branch EAD has empowered me personally to see to it that no fucking terrorists infiltrate our country and try to take a giant shit all over its liberties!"

"Well that sounds good," I said, raising my voice to a level not quite as loud as Special Agent Turdington. Psychology plays a big part in sales and one trick is to speak in a similar manner as your prospect, but stopping short of exactly mimicking him. "Now, Ted, can you tell me what that has to do with me?"

"You've been tagged, my friend. You are a veritable person of interest. You won't be able to shake the dew off your dick without it being analyzed by every agent in counterterrorism. Now what do you think of that?"

"I'm still wondering why. I have nothing to do with terrorism. I'm an agent and registered representative for the National American Life Insurance Company of Maryland."

"Yeah, I know what your cover is. Let's face it, buddy. You have been officially neutralized as of now by Special Agent Turdington. Tell me where you went this afternoon."

I wanted to say I went to a secret location and shook the dew off my dick, but thought better of it. "I went to my office in Beltsville. I worked on a financial-freedom package for a gentleman who works in government and would like to retire comfortably by the age of 60."

"Do you take me for an idiot?"

"Ted, what kind of a question is that?"

"Go ahead. Take a swing at me."

"What?" I said as the bizarre conversation took an even

more bizarre turn.

"Make my job easy. Take a swing at me."

"No, Ted, I'm not going to take a swing at you. But what I would like to do is talk to you about starting up a college funding account for the kids with a special life insurance rider in case anything happens to you before the account is built up."

"In case anything happens to me? What's going to happen to me, Ahkbar? You going to call in the jihadi suicide bombers? Huh?"

"Can I reach into my jacket and give you my card?"

"No!" he yelled, sounding like he'd damaged a vocal cord. "What I want you to do is become the last digit of Pi down at Gitmo!"

"What? Pi? But they're closing Gitmo."

"That's what you think, pal," he said and then reached into his own jacket. "I'm giving you my card. If you decide you want to get anything off your chest, call this number. It will be the smartest thing you ever did."

I took the card and waited. Special Agent Turdington just stared at me. "Can I go now?" I said finally.

"You're free to go." He didn't move. He stayed and watched me as I went into my house.

7

The next day I met my friend Julia for lunch. She was the one who'd rekindled The Theory with her revelation of John Dean's death, the cause of which had still not been officially given. The latest was that it could be weeks before the medical examiner released anything definitive.

Julia and I had become an item shortly after I'd separated from my wife. Our intimate relations ran their course after a few months, but we had remained friends. We dished gossip, talked politics, went to plays and art films together. Without a permanent female presence in my life, Julia provided the feminine influence.

I determined not to tell her about Todd Manderville or my visit to the Secret Service or my run-in with Special Agent Turdington. For her own protection I didn't want her to know anything. So the conversation was largely about Amber.

"So I think I'm hot for a client," I told her.

"Oh Hank, you're not serious."

"And she's married."

"Get out," Julia said and took a sip off her herbal iced tea. "So do you know what she thinks of you?"

"She seems very eager for me to help her with things."

"Uh oh."

"What do you mean, 'uh oh'?"

"Hank, if she's asking you to help her with things it means she's interested in you."

"You think?"

"Hank, don't do it. She's married, and a client. You could get in a lot of trouble."

"You don't know the half of it."

"Why, there's more?"

"Not that I can talk about now."

Then Julia asked a loaded question. "Do you think she might just be interested in you because she's mad at her husband?"

"Um, that might have a little to do with it."

"Hank, that might have more to do with it than you think."

I knew some women could get mad at their husband for spending too much time watching TV, or going out with the guys, or looking at other women. But being away from the house too much to work on a presidential assassination plot was a new one on me.

"Just be careful, Hank. It's not worth the risk."

"Julia, my business is risk."

Which was true, though the actuaries at NALIC of Maryland would tell you that the business isn't in taking risks, but in managing risks. It's similar to a Las Vegas casino. Are they taking a risk when they leave it to chance whether the customers walk away with all their money? Of course they are. But the laws of probability hold as firm for casinos as they do for life insurance companies. If you do a volume business you can fairly accurately predict what percentage of your customers will take your money at any given time.

I knew what Julia was talking about, but what was I risking at this point? If anything happened between me and Amber I didn't think the managing partner at my office would care. He was himself at that moment carrying on an affair with a married woman in data entry. Todd would mind, if he found out. But he was away for large chunks of time at Fort Myer and the cemetery. If Amber was right and he got himself into a dangerous mission where he could be killed, that would play itself out fairly soon. If she was wrong and nothing happened, how long would it be before she let the policy lapse? She wasn't going to keep paying those premiums—which increased annually—for long.

Furthermore, I felt I was managing the risk by investigating this story of Amber's myself. The sooner I found out which side of the veracity fence it fell on, the sooner I'd have my answer whether I'd be sleeping with a millionaire or having my commission revoked because of a policy lapse within 12 months. Not to mention, I'd probably investigate this thing anyway just because I was so damn curious about it all.

That being the other element of the risk, I'd gotten the Secret Service interested in me, the FBI interested in me, all these people interested in me. For someone specializing in outside sales, getting people interested in you is what you want. It's part of the job. I could see myself doing mortgage-payoff plans for half the staff at the Federal Bureau of Investigation. A mother lode of quality prospects is all any decent salesperson needs.

8

I called Private Peter Huguenot of the 3rd U.S. Infantry Regiment. A fellow Tomb guard, he was on the list of referrals I'd obtained from Todd. I asked if I could meet him in the cemetery. I said I had curiosity as a tourist and wanted to get a picture for my niece— though I really wanted to see if there was anything about the place that made it attractive for recruiting, shall we say, secret-mission specialists. He said he didn't think we could meet there, but he would ask his superiors. When I called later to confirm he sounded surprised that his commander had okayed my visit.

When one approaches the Memorial Amphitheater at Arlington National Cemetery it's like walking out of 21st century Virginia in the United States and into the Athens of ancient Greece. It is a 5,000-seat neoclassical edifice of bright white marble. Dozens of Doric columns arranged concentrically inside a circular arcade meet at an imposing stage made entirely of the same pure white marble. Above the west entrance is inscribed "DULCE ET DECORUM EST PRO PATRIA MORI," a Latin quote from Horace that means "It is sweet and fitting to die for one's country." Behind the stage is the Memorial Display Room. Continue out the front of the Display Room and you descend a wide marble staircase to the Tomb of the Unknowns. This is the most sacred military site in the nation.

It is here that the sentinels of the Tomb walk their patrols day and night, 365 days a year. When not walking they stay in the Tomb Guard Quarters, located below the Memorial Display Room. I met with Private Huguenot in the quarters, and, like Todd, he seemed as normal as they come, very natural and engaged with his surroundings. I did my job and went through the usual process, though my heart, perhaps, wasn't fully in it. Part of me felt I had bigger fish to fry. I found that Private Huguenot had been married just under a year and he and his wife were expecting a child. So I talked with him about additional life insurance and a college-funding plan. I said I'd put together several options back at the office and come back with some affordable solutions for him and his wife. Then I said, due to the nature of his occupation, I had to ask a few questions that my underwriting department required me to ask.

"There's no need to be specific," I said, "but has anyone ever approached you about becoming part of a special, secret mission?"

"I don't think I'd be able to tell you if that did happen. But nobody ever has, so there's your answer."

"So that's your answer because you can't tell me or because no one's ever approached you?"

"No one's approached me."

"Okay, are Tomb guards sometimes asked to perform special missions?"

"It depends on what you mean by special missions. Our duty includes providing security in the District region when called upon."

WILLIAM A. MAYS

"I guess I mean anything in addition to what you're normally expected to do. Any unusual missions that are not spelled out when you join up."

"No, I don't think there's anything like that."

"But you guys do protect the president from time to time, is that right?"

"That depends on what you mean by 'you guys,'" he began. "There are a number of different battalions and companies that make up the Old Guard. We're Echo Company. Our main duty is ceremonial. We only see the president during official ceremonial events like when a foreign leader comes to the District on a state visit, or during the laying of the wreath on holidays."

"Right, that would be Memorial Day here at the Tomb."

"Memorial Day, Veterans Day, Easter. The president doesn't always come to every one. Memorial Day is usually when he's here."

I had to pause and think for a moment. If Todd's story, as told by Amber, were true then this would be the only point of connection between Todd and President Obama. It's possible his handlers might pluck him out of Echo Company and put him where needed at the appropriate time, but I wondered...

"When the president comes here for the Memorial Day ceremony, you would say this is a pretty safe and secure environment for him, wouldn't you?"

"Absolutely."

"The United States military and security services have complete control of this place."

"That's correct."

"Interesting," I said, letting my mind wander.

"So," Private Huguenot said, breaking my reverie, "how much did you say this would cost?"

"Hm? Oh, well within your budget that we discussed. But let me crunch the numbers back at the office and I can come back with specific plans that you can choose from. Have you ever heard the name Artemus Schreckengost?"

"Sir?"

"Artemus Schreckengost. I heard that he works here at the cemetery."

"No, I'm not familiar with that name."

"Okay, I was hoping I might be able to see him too as long as I'm up here. You see, my business runs on referrals and I'd appreciate it if you could give me the names of ten friends and family members...."

I left Arlington National Cemetery with more questions than when I'd come. If the military and the Secret Service thought the attempt on President Obama's life might happen at the Tomb, then they must have known they were dealing with elements within their own government. No one else could get in there and get close enough, unless it was done by air. But if it was to be done by air, then why that location? Why not any number of other places? And if by air, then what could Todd possibly be able to do? Unless, again, he were to be removed from his normal post and assigned somewhere else entirely.

That night I was trying to stay awake during the Colbert Report when I heard a strange noise. You hear a lot of noises during the course of a day or night and you get pretty familiar with which noises belong where—and what noises indicate a possible problem. It was that kind of noise. It was the sound of mechanical work being done, but much closer than it should have been. Close enough to be on my property in the vicinity of my car.

I jumped up and looked out the window. I couldn't quite see anything, so I put on my bathrobe and went to the front door. Taking a deep breath I opened it quickly and went out toward the car. I saw a young black male, a teenager I thought, poke his head up out of my car from the opened driver-side door. He ducked and said something. Then another black teenager appeared from underneath the car and the two of them ran off.

I got my flashlight and gave the car a going over. I looked underneath and inside, even under the hood, which I didn't think they'd opened. Everything looked fine. Whatever it was they were trying to do, it looked like I interrupted them. But what were they trying to do? Certain people knew by this time I was snooping around probably where I shouldn't have been. If there really was a plot to assassinate President Obama, it's possible they might try to do something to me—like sabotage my car, for instance. But black kids? I knew this was a new, multi-cultural world. But were black kids really the new G. Gordon Liddy and E. Howard Hunt? I didn't know what to think.

I wasn't racist. I could say I was a white man who had dated black women. Although, as we know, just because a white man hooks up with a black woman it doesn't mean he's not racist. In any case, I chalked it up to a simple neighborhood crime. Nothing was stolen; nothing was broken—they must have had a jimmy to get the door open. That was one reason why I didn't call the police. The other reason was: the racism inherent in assuming that black kids couldn't be part of a vast, well-funded conspiracy to assassinate the leader of the free world notwithstanding, there was the thought in the back of my mind what if they were? A call to the police only makes people like that angry. People like that move the police around like pawns on a chess board. No, I had to keep searching and find out for myself what was going on.

I checked my car again the next day when it was light outside. Again, everything looked okay, though I still cringed when I turned the key in the ignition switch. This was my first twinge of paranoia. Somebody like Special Agent Turdington I could handle. Not knowing whether there was a bomb in my car was another matter. But I was a life insurance agent, and a good one. People like me drive through paranoia, depression, bad luck, and the whole panoply of life's slings and arrows like an airboat through a swamp. You do not hold us back, ever.

9

There was beginning to be a delay in the processing of the Mandervilles' insurance policy, so I called underwriting to find out what was happening. It turned out when they interviewed Todd he apparently told them he actually had ridden a motorcycle within the past two years. To the casual observer this might not seem like earth-shattering news. But to underwriting it was a reason to do further investigation to see if Todd was likely to be riding motorcycles in the future, at which point he would be assigned a lower rating with a correspondingly higher premium.

We agents don't love telling clients that their approval will be delayed another month and that their premium will be higher than we quoted. But it was all in a day's work. I called Amber with the news and an interesting thing happened that a) I'm glad happened on my TracFone, and b) I could rationalize as just a hypothetical, not an actual deal. I told Amber about the delay, the motorcycle situation and the possible increase in premium and she said, "I don't want this policy declined. I'll give you a million dollars out of the payout if you can get this to go through."

Now, I hadn't told her the policy might be declined. I told

her underwriting was investigating. Unless Todd was racing motorcycles for a living the policy would be approved, just with a higher premium. But once again, Amber gave me a moral pause. Should I take advantage of this misunderstanding? I ended up telling her I would talk to underwriting and make sure the policy went through, but I did not acknowledge what she had said about the million dollars. This way I could tell her later that I'd bent over backwards to get the policy approved, at which point a premium increase would seem like small potatoes. And if she wanted to give me $1,000,000 in the event Todd died, well, I'd fall off that bridge when I came to it.

Normally, agents don't contact the underwriting department to pressure them into approving policies or giving better ratings. It's not allowed. If underwriting had to deal with calls from agents about getting their applications approved, no actual work would ever get done. Fortunately for me, Richard W. Fox, the managing partner of the Beltsville general office of the National American Life Insurance Company of Maryland, treated all rules and regulations like suggestions. I told him my client was balking at the possibility of a lower rating, and I needed this case to go through so I could hit my monthly goal. Rich Fox got on the phone to his person on the inside at underwriting. "Dolores, Rich. Congratulations on Debbie's graduation. How are the other kids? .... That's great. Frank must be very happy. .... The puppy is doing wonderfully, thank you. You picked out the best of the litter for me, and I appreciate that. .... Dolores, when was the last time I asked you for a favor?"

Rich Fox went on to tell Dolores he had an agent who might be in the running for Million Dollar Round Table membership for the first time. "Pirandello says we just need a few more agents," Fox told her, "and we could challenge New York

Life this year. ....." Fox laughed at something Dolores said. "Yeah, I know. Sounded like bullshit to me too." He winked at me. "Anyway, do you think you could help me out?"

Dolores told Rich Fox she'd look into it and call back later. When she did, it turned out underwriting had decided Todd wasn't a risk to be doing much motorcycle riding, so the policy was approved as originally presented to the client anyway. No arm twisting was even necessary. But as the dutiful, customer-is-always-right, value-added guy I was, I could honestly report to Amber that I had made the effort.

When the policy came in I made an appointment with Amber to deliver it—a policy-delivery date, it turned out, that would live in infamy. She met me at my office in the evening, and we went to the same conference room where I'd first interviewed her. I told her I'd used my influence with the underwriting department to get her a great deal, and she seemed very appreciative of that. Then, as with any policy delivery, I went over the provisions with the client. She showed no concern about the premium increasing over time or the option to convert the policy into permanent insurance later on. She was most interested in making sure the face amount and beneficiary information were correct, along with the procedure for filing a claim. She signed the receipt and that was that.

We looked at each other for a moment. I felt a tug when I thought this might be the last time I'd see her for a while. Then she said, "You know, I don't know what I'm going to do if anything happens to Todd. I mean, even now I get lonely. He's away from home a lot and we don't get that close anymore. But if he wasn't around anymore I'd need someone to help me with things. I don't have anybody."

My momma didn't raise no dummies, as the saying goes. I knew what Amber was up to. But knowing what someone is up to and deciding whether you'll go along with it are two different things. She looked just as hot as ever. The first time I saw her I felt a bit of the thunderbolt. And the way she was looking at me now and the tone in her voice made her hard to resist. There's got to be something in the biological makeup of people that makes women know instinctively what they can do with their voice and the subtlest of body language to turn on the switch deep inside the male psyche. I did, however, believe in free will, and a voice in my head said to me, "Stick to business." But there was another voice that did not deal in complexities; to this voice most choices were simple and obvious. This voice said, "Damn. Dude. C'mon!" So I ended the policy-delivery meeting by asking Amber, "May I kiss you?"

She nodded and I got up and went around to her. While standing I leaned over and kissed her. Her lips felt great and we kissed for a long time like that. I asked her to stand up and I began kissing her neck while I caressed her. Things barreled forward from there and soon Amber was sitting on the conference table. I had her dress up, got her underwear down, and went straight down to give her a lengthy session of oral sex. While I did, I thought about how the NALIC of Maryland Beltsville General Office conference table had seen a lot of strange things, but I wondered if this was a first.

She enjoyed what I was doing, and after a while she pulled me up to her. "Go to the middle of the table," I said, and she moved to the center of the big table next to the teleconference speaker. I climbed up with her and dropped my pants. "How are you about unprotected sex?" I asked.

"I'm okay with it," she said. "I'm on the pill."

We went at it on the table; the skin on the back of Amber's

ass squeaked against the polished wood. When she orgasmed, Amber sounded like someone had just stabbed her in the gut. The noise of our lovemaking was such that if there had been anyone else in the office we'd certainly have been found out.

Afterwards, we lay on the table for a while. "Has Todd told you anything else about his mission or the plot?" I asked her.

"Nothing. I don't know any more than what I told you."

I didn't want to tell her the extent of my snooping. My obsession with conspiracy theories was my own issue and I didn't need to involve her. My interest in Amber Manderville was sexual, with a chance at a monetary reward. But since, so far, she was the only source of evidence that a plan to kill President Obama existed, I wanted to keep her close and honest. "How can you be so sure," I asked her, "that Todd will actually be caught up in this assassination?"

"Everything," Amber said, "and I mean everything Todd has ever told me has been the truth. If he says something is going to happen, then it happens."

I rubbed the back of her neck as she spoke.

"That's why I got so freaked out," she continued. "Todd said he'd probably be killed doing this thing. You don't know Todd, but he never guesses. If he says 'probably' he means 'definitely.'"

Amber and I got up and got dressed. I told her I'd like to see her again, but I didn't know when. She said she would call me. I looked around the room to make sure everything was in order, but chose to leave the conference table as it was—splashed with bodily fluids and all. We were having a meeting the next morning and I wanted to sit there and have a private little joke.

I went to bed that night feeling pretty satisfied. I'd delivered a policy that came with a nice commission and had sex with a beautiful woman on top of my office's conference-room table. I'd say overall it had been a good day. Then, at about 5:30 in the morning my TracFone rang. The ID said "private call," which puzzled me since I hadn't given my number to anyone whose own number was unlisted. When I answered I heard a voice that sounded vaguely like Special Agent Turdington's, but I wasn't sure. "Hank, listen carefully," the voice said. "Julia Scheider is being held."

"What?" I muttered. "Who is this?"

"Julia is being held temporarily. Do you understand?"

"No, I don't. Who is holding Julia?" Then the phone disconnected.

I called Julia's number and there was no answer, though that didn't necessarily mean anything at that time of the morning. Julia had no problem calling other people at all hours, but she rarely answered her own phone before 7:00am. Then I called Julia's mom, who lived nearby, and asked if she could check on her daughter.

"What is it, Hank? What's the matter?"

"I don't know, Peggy. It seems she was out last night closing the bars and I think she ended up with an ex-con. We have a system where she calls me by five in the morning if everything's alright. But today she didn't."

"Oh, Hank!" she said. I knew that would get her going. I didn't know what had happened to Julia, but it seemed like time was of the essence, and I wasn't going to tell Julia's mom what my real suspicions were. If everything was okay, Julia and I would have a good laugh over this later. Well, I would anyway.

Peggy called back after she went to Julia's house. She found the door closed, but unlocked, and when she went in she found everything normal except there was no Julia. At that point, I decided I had 48 hours to find out what had happened. First, because the sooner Julia was found the better, but second, though Peggy had said she was calling the police as soon as she was off the phone with me, in a missing-person case the police generally don't get involved until 48 hours have elapsed. At that point they were sure to start asking questions that went beyond the subject of picking up ex-cons in bars.

I was despondent, but determined. Something had happened to one of my best friends, but worse was the feeling that it had been my fault. If I hadn't gone poking around in the wrong places, maybe Julia would still be around.

I found Ted Turdington's card and called him. "Did you call me early this morning?" I asked.

"Mr. Stafford, what a surprise. Tell me what's new in your life."

"Ted, I was thinking you could tell me what was new in my life. Like, for instance, what's going on with certain people I know."

"You'll have to give me names, smart guy. 'People' is a general term."

"Okay, where's Julia?"

There was a pause. "'Where's Julia?'" he repeated back. "Sounds like you've got a problem you need help with. Great. Here I am waiting for a call from you to discuss some real issues. And the only time you call is when you have a mess you need me to clean up. What has become of our relationship, Mr. Stafford?"

"Ted, did you have anything to do with it?"

"You should come in and talk with me. There's a place in southeast DC where we could meet."

I wasn't getting anywhere with Special Agent Turdington. I didn't want to travel all the way to southeast DC—and why he wanted to meet there was puzzling—just to listen to him make more snide remarks and not provide any information. I told him to call me back when he had some ransom demands.

"Do call again, Mr. Stafford. I enjoy our conversations," I heard him say as I hung up the phone.

10

I left my house to get some air and try to settle my mind. But as I walked down the sidewalk I sensed someone following me. I stopped and turned around. Standing there was a white male in his early 20s. I wasn't startled because he looked completely harmless and was smiling at me. He wore a red T-shirt with a black, hooded sweatshirt and jeans that didn't fit his hips quite right, like they were actually for a woman. "Hi," he said.

"Hello," I replied. He didn't say anything; he just kept smiling. I noticed the artwork on his sweatshirt. It appeared to be from a woodcut and depicted a person drowning in a stormy sea. At the top of the picture was the word "THRICE."

"Thrice," I said, attempting to start conversation. "That's a very interesting sweater."

"Do you know them?" the strange young man asked. "You should."

"Really? Why is that?"

"Dude. Beltsville! You live in Beltsville."

"Okay, you know something about me. Now, who are you?"

"My name's Tyler."

I shook his hand. "Well, hello, Tyler. What can I do for you?"

"You don't know? The Illusion of Safety... The Beltsville Crucible. Dude, Thrice!" He pointed at his sweatshirt. I looked puzzled. "You don't know them? They recorded The Illusion of Safety in Beltsville. The Beltsville Crucible is a song."

"Oh, okay," I said.

"What about Thursday?"

"What's happening on Thursday?"

"No, dude. They're another band."

"Oh, rock bands." I said. "Okay, well, I've got to get going." I started back down the sidewalk. But young Tyler kept right along with me.

"What about Boy Sets Fire, The Used, Avail, Dillinger Escape Plan, the almighty Snapcase? You know them? Dude, you must have heard of My Chemical Romance."

"No, I'm sorry. That's not my area of musical expertise."

"Hardcore, dude. You're in the region where it was invented. Minor Threat, Ian MacKaye. Plus, you know, Bad Brains are good too. I just like to X up."

I remained silent and kept walking. Then Tyler said, "I think he's a Manchurian Candidate."

"Who," I said, "Ian MacKaye?"

"Nope. Todd Manderville."

I stopped walking. How did this strange kid know about me, Todd, and—apparently—the plot too? But he wasn't done yet. "I mean," he continued, "'please pay to the order of Artemus Schreckengost'? What is that? Did you know they found the phrase 'please pay to the order' scribbled all over Sirhan Sirhan's notebook? They're not very original are they?"

"How do you know all this?"

"Amber told me."

"What?" I said, incensed. I thought I was the only one Amber had told. And who was this kid? If she told him, who else was she going around telling? I felt like she was cheating on me. "How do you know Amber?"

"I pick up my brother at the school where she works. She's his teacher. We get to talking sometimes and I told her how I'm the area expert on assassination conspiracies. That's when she told me about her husband."

I grumbled.

"Maybe she thought I could help."

So now Amber was cheating on me with some freakish 20-year old. Maybe not in a sexual way, but damn it, I wanted to be the one to expose the conspirators to the world. Now I had to compete with Mr. Thrice Beltsville here. "You know what, Tyler?" I said. "It's all a hoax. There is no assassination plot. Amber's pulling your leg."

"Dude, you're not serious."

"As a heart attack. Amber and Todd like to play games on people. They're like swingers, except instead of wife swapping they're into messing with people's minds."

"No," Tyler lamented. "So I guess that Turdington guy is just doing that to get his jollies off."

"Doing what? What do you know about him?"

"He showed me his FBI ID card. Dude, it's a fake."

"Are you telling me...."

"Yes. Ted Turdington is not an FBI agent."

He went on to say that his dad worked for the FBI, that Tyler could tell a fake ID when he saw one. And not just because he knew what his dad's looked like. "Before I turned 18 I had to get good at making fake IDs 'cause not all the shows I went to were all ages. It's just like the Secret Service agents in Dealy Plaza after JFK was killed," he continued. "A half dozen people, including two different cops, saw them there flashing their badges. All fakes. There were no Secret Service agents in Dealy Plaza after the assassination." He said he hadn't told his dad yet about his run-in with Turdington. He wanted to handle the investigation himself and not let the FBI take it away from him. I guessed I could identify with that, but it still didn't change the fact I didn't want any competition. And anyway, this Tyler kid seemed a little unstable. I couldn't be sure of the accuracy of what he told me or if he could be trusted.

I made a remark about how it was great to have someone else on the trail of the assassins and we should keep in contact. Then I told him I forgot something back at my house and had to get going.

I got in my car and drove straight to Amber's place in Wheaton. I didn't call first since the TracFone seemed compromised, and when she answered her door I put my finger up to my lips in a "shhh" gesture. "Come with me," I whispered. I drove her to Kensington Heights Park, rebuffing any attempt by her to start a conversation. We walked deep into the park among the trees, and I finally spoke.

"What are you doing telling some weird kid all about Todd's mission? This is very sensitive stuff, Amber. You can't be telling everyone you meet."

"I haven't been telling everyone I meet. And why are you acting like a crazy person and won't let me talk?"

"I'm not crazy. It's just that the Secret Service and Special Agent Turdington are on to me, though Turdington may not be a real FBI agent, and I think he might have kidnapped my friend, and I think black kids may have bugged my car."

Amber stared at me in silence. Finally she said, "I thought I could trust you, Hank. You seemed real serious. But now it's like you're losing it."

"Okay, okay," I said. "This investigation is just making me crazy. It's alright."

"What investigation, Hank? What are you doing?"

I'd let that slip. I'd been keeping that part from Amber, but the stress of the moment caused me to drop my guard. "Okay," I said, "I've been looking into a few things just to see how likely it is that Todd might actually be in danger, that's all. I wouldn't want to see him get hurt, because, you know, it would hurt you."

Amber's tone softened. "Oh, honey," she said, "that's sweet." She put her hands around the back of my neck, her wrists resting on my shoulders. "But you don't have to worry about me. I'll be fine."

I put my hands around her waist. She felt so good.

"It's good that you're looking into this," she said. "I want to be sure if Todd is really going to die or not. And you should let Tyler help you. He's got connections and he knows a lot."

I kissed her on the neck and she put her arms all the way around me.

"So if you find out Todd's not really in danger," she said, "what are you going to do?"

By now I was holding her close; my hand massaged her backside. "Breathe a sigh of relief," I said.

Amber untucked my shirt and slipped her hands underneath. "Won't you be disappointed?"

I kissed her and we kissed deeply for a while. Finally I said, "Disappointed about what?"

"The million dollars."

I'd started unbuttoning her shirt and didn't quite comprehend what she was saying at first. "What million dollars?"

"The million I promised you out of Todd's insurance policy."

"Oh, that million," I said as I undid her bra and leaned my head down while Amber dug her fingers into my hair.

As I began suckling her breast she said between little gasps, "Maybe if Todd doesn't die the way he said, maybe there's another way. Another way we might be able to get him to go."

"Go where?" I said while holding on gently with my teeth.

"You know. Go away. You know. Die."

She was rubbing my head and panting and starting to squirm. I undid her pants and we laid on the ground. We had sex there on the fresh spring grass next to a tree in the middle of Kensington Heights Park.

My mind cleared as I drove Amber home afterward. But I didn't revisit the comment she'd made about Todd. In my business sometimes if you ignore problems they really do go away. I felt so sure a plot to kill President Obama existed that I remained focused on that. If I could expose the perpetrators, there would be enough fame and praise and money to go around—just the insurance business alone I could generate as the man who saved the president would get me MDRT status, if not Court of the Table—making Amber's offer of $1,000,000 moot.

11

Amber and I both wanted to know what was really going on with Todd and his "mission," though we each had our very different reasons. I decided to trust her and bring Tyler into my confidence, reasoning that he already knew enough that he could cause trouble and better to have him inside peeing out than outside peeing in, as they say. I bought a new TracFone and called him.

"Dude! You're stuck."

"What?" I said, thinking I understood Tyler's words, but the music in the background was so loud I wasn't sure.

"You called me. You must be stuck."

"Tyler, I can't hear you. Turn down the music!"

"Dude, it's Converge! You don't turn down Converge."

The music—if you could call it that—consisted of vocals not sung but shrieked over dissonant chords and manic drumming. If "Reefer Madness" were filmed today, this is the music they'd be playing. "Tyler," I yelled, "you must be high on drugs!"

"No way, dude. I haven't broken my edge in four years! I just listen to Converge 'cause I like 'em."

This was a segment of society, I decided, that I would never understand, so I tried to stick to the point. "I'm coming to pick you up. Stay there!" I shouted. He either said "yup" or "what?" I wasn't sure. But I drove to the address Amber gave me and got Tyler.

He lived in an illegal basement studio apartment that smelled like mildew. I knew Ted Turdington—and who knows who else—knew about him, so I wanted to get him away from his home. After seeing it, though, I decided I was doing him a favor.

"Do you have a CD player in your car?" he asked.

"Yes," I said, "just come on." He gathered a handful of CDs and we were on our way. First, I parked my car in a McDonald's lot. Then we took the bus to a car rental place, where I rented a black Cadillac Escalade. They were having a special deal on those things, so that's what I got.

As soon as we got in and started driving, Tyler held up a CD and said "Unsane. Scattered, Smothered and Covered. An all-time classic." The cover showed a blood-soaked pillow over the head of a dead victim with a ball-peen hammer lying nearby. He started to put the CD in the player.

"Wait a minute, Tyler," I said, grabbing his arm. "I need to talk to you about a serious matter right now. Maybe we can listen to some of your music later."

"Okay, how about Poison The Well."

"What? No. Now listen. You've got to tell me everything you know about the plot to kill President Obama."

"Okay, so Amber's husband Todd is a Manchurian Candidate, right? He's all programmed to shoot Obama as he's laying the wreath at the Tomb of the Unknowns in Arlington Cemetery on Memorial Day."

"Wait. Stop right there. What makes you think he's a Manchurian Candidate? Why couldn't he be a secret operative working for the good guys? What if he's part of a government operation to find and neutralize a different part of the government that's trying to carry out the assassination?"

"Dude, you got it all wrong. He responds to coded prompts planted in his mind through hypnosis. He's a trusted member of the Army's DC unit. He's going to be within a few feet of Obama on Memorial Day. This guy is the most closely guarded president in history. This is the only way they can get at him."

"Tyler, I hate to break it to you, but there's no such thing as a Manchurian Candidate. The CIA's experiments in that area went nowhere. The outcomes were too unpredictable. They stopped that program over 30 years ago."

"And where'd you get that information from? The CIA? Isn't it in their interest to say they stopped a program when they really didn't?"

"Have you told Amber this theory of yours?"

"No, dude. I didn't want her to get more scared than she already is."

"Okay, let's say for the sake of argument that Todd is on the wrong side in this. Do any of the good guys in the government know about it? I mean besides Ted Turdington, but you think he's one of them anyway."

"No, I don't think he's real FBI. The dude's got major circuit damage in his brain."

"Your dad works for the FBI. Couldn't he find out?"

"What do you think, they hand out lists of everybody who works for the FBI to all the employees?"

"Alright, so what did Turdington say to you?"

"He said a lot of crazy things. He wanted to know if I knew you. I said 'No, dude. I don't know any Hank Stafford.' And that's when he went psycho. I loved how he started acting like the sheriff of DC. He said 'you've got till noon on Friday to get out of town.'

He said 'I want you in Reagan Airport and on a plane out of Washington.'"

"By noon Friday?"

"That's what he said."

I called Peggy to check the status at her end. "Hank, I still don't know where she is," she said. "The police said I had to wait, but I'm about to lose my mind. I don't know what to do. I told them that and I wouldn't let them go until I got an answer."

This I believed. Julia's mom was the kind of person who once she set her mind to something, it was a foregone conclusion that it would get done. I almost wanted to tell her everything and get her on the case—in which case it might be solved overnight—but the fewer people getting involved the better. I knew she would work the normal-channel angle until it was worked into the ground, so I left her to it.

"So I demanded to speak to someone higher up," she said, "and first they disconnected me, and when I called back they put me on hold for 20 minutes."

"So what happened?"

"Well finally I got someone who was much more pleasant and understanding. He said more help is coming. He said a special missing-person investigator is flying into National Airport today at twelve something. He even gave me the flight number."

"Reagan National Airport. That's very interesting. Do you happen to remember the flight?"

"I wrote it down. It's Continental flight 1058 from Houston."

That was an interesting coincidence. There was a missing-person expert arriving at Reagan Airport at the same time that Ted Turdington told Tyler to be there to get out of town. I looked at my dashboard clock. If Tyler were to follow Turdington's directions he had one hour to get to the airport. So I got on the Beltway.

Keeping my promise to Tyler, I let him play some of his music on the trip. We had the mellow strains of Kill Your Idols blasting out our Escalade windows as we sped toward the airport. After pulling into a short-term parking space I turned off the car. Finally, there was silence. "Tyler," I said, "I think it's safe to say I now have permanent damage to my hearing."

"Don't tell me you didn't like that."

"No, Tyler. I have to be honest. That's not my kind of music."

"So, what do you rock out to?"

"I guess you could say I like classic rock."

"Are you talking about Black Sabbath classic rock or Rush classic rock or Steve Miller classic rock, because if it's the last one I don't know if we can be friends."

I really did not want to be arguing about this subject. "Let's just stick to business," I said, "and we'll be fine."

We went to Terminal B and waited for flight 1058. Tyler bought some paper and a marker and made a sign to hold up for the arriving passengers that said "MISSING PERSON INVESTIGATOR DUDE." His heart was in the right place, but I had other ideas. When the flight landed I went to a customer service desk and told them my companion whom I'd come there with had wandered off. He had the beginnings of Alzheimer's disease and could quickly become disoriented without me, so would they please be sure to page "Mr. Artemus Schreckengost" as many times as they could.

I stood off to the side and watched as the passengers filed into the terminal, the page for Artemus Schreckengost wafting through the air above them. Nobody seemed to pay the slightest attention to either the page or to Tyler's sign. Then, finally, I saw a woman walk over to the customer service desk. In response to something she said, the customer-service agent pointed in my direction. She turned, and I couldn't tell if she was looking at me or past me. But she left the desk and headed in the direction of Terminal C. I left Tyler at the gate and followed the mystery person. Suddenly, another person approached from my left. "Mr. Stafford," he said. "I'm glad to see you."

I turned and saw Private Peter Huguenot of the Tomb guards. I looked over his shoulder and caught a glimpse of the mystery person going into the Cibo Bistro and Wine Bar. "Private Huguenot, nice to see you. What are you doing here?"

"I'm on leave. I just found out. I got my orders for a two-week leave, so I'm going home today."

"Two weeks. That runs through Memorial Day, doesn't it?"

"Yes, sir. So I'm going to have to reschedule our appointment."

"Oh, okay. That's fine," I said as I frequently peeked over at the wine bar's entrance. "Tell you what: enjoy yourself, have a good time with your family. And we'll get together when you come back."

"Okay, Mr. Stafford. That sounds great."

I bade Private Huguenot bon voyage and went straight into the wine bar. Looking around, I saw a few other people, and then spotted the mystery woman sitting at the bar. I approached and asked her if she'd seen anybody who looked disoriented. I described him as being about so high wearing a something or other. And his name was "Artemus Schreckengost."

She said she hadn't seen who I was talking about, but then added, "Can I buy you a drink?"

I was probably acting as if I needed a mellowing agent, but this was unexpected. A woman I'd never met before offering to buy me a drink was a rare occurrence. The last time it happened I was in a bar on Eighth Ave in Manhattan. It did not end well. After a pause I said, "Right now I can't see any conflict of interest. So I'll accept your offer."

"Conflict of interest?" she inquired.

"Yes. Your buying me a drink can't be considered an improper gift because we don't know each other and have never had any dealings together. No quid pro quo exists."

"I see," she said, and we ordered drinks. I got a sauvignon blanc and the lady got a white wine spritzer.

"The only problem I can see when a lady offers to buy me drink is I don't get to use one of my famous pick-up lines."

"Oh? Well, can I hear one?"

"Sure. This one always reels them in: 'Hello, ma'am. You seem to be a non-smoking female under the age of 35. I bet I could get you permanent life insurance coverage for about a dollar a day.'"

She laughed. "Let me guess. You sell life insurance."

"As long as you bring it up, yes, I've secured the financial futures of countless families and business owners by now."

"Well, if I ever need life insurance I'll know who to call."

I took a business card from my pocket and handed it to her.

"Henry A. 'Hank' Stafford, it's a pleasure to meet you."

"Likewise. And with whom do I have the pleasure of sharing drinks today?"

"I'm Susan. Susan Underhill."

I offered my hand and we shook. "Are you traveling somewhere?"

"No, I'm waiting for a flight to come in."

"Oh, is your husband on it?"

"No, my mother. I live alone and she's coming to visit for a while."

"Well, Miss Underhill, thank you so much for the glass of

wine. I really do need to get going, but I would like to make an appointment to see you again and maybe talk about some financial planning."

"Wait," she said. "You know that man you were looking for? He did come in here."

"Did he? What did he look like?"

"Oh, he was about so high and wore a something or other. I think he saw you coming, and he gave me this to give you." Susan pulled out a piece of paper and gave it to me. "I didn't give it to you before because you seemed like a nice person to spend some time with."

I read the slip of paper. It said "Come to the Washington Monument tomorrow evening. I have something you might find interesting."

"The only thing that would make this complete, Miss Underhill, is if it had your phone number on it." She told me her number, but asked me to write it down on a different piece of paper.

I went back out to find Tyler, but he was no longer standing by the passenger exit with his sign. Returning to the customer service desk, I asked a) if anyone had answered the Artemus Schreckengost page and b) if they'd seen where Tyler went. The man at the desk answered in the negative to the first question, but regarding Tyler he said he'd been led away by some TSA agents.

"Oh, great," I said. "Do you know where they take people who get detained?"

"No," said the man, "but I can direct you to the TSA supervisor."

I found my way to the TSA office and pleaded to see the young man they'd just brought in. I said he was my nephew and that his mother would be worried about him. The officer I spoke with took my name and told me to wait. I sat there for almost an hour. There were no magazines or TV to look at, just walls painted a washed-out yellowish green.

Finally, the officer I'd spoken with came back. "He says you're not his uncle."

"Thanks, Tyler," I muttered to myself. "Alright, that's true. I'm not..." I began when the officer cut me off.

"It doesn't matter. We checked him out. We have no reason to hold him. Just don't bring him back here again unless he's getting on a flight."

"Can I ask why you folks detained him in the first place?"

"He was behaving erratically in the middle of the terminal, making physical gestures that were upsetting to the other customers."

"Really."

"We already explained to him he's not to do that again and if he does he'll be arrested and charged with disturbing the peace."

I promised to make Tyler stop doing whatever it was he was doing and take him off the property immediately. Shortly, he emerged from the back. "Mr. Stafford, dude!"

As I escorted him back out to the car I asked him to explain what it was he was doing.

"Dancing, dude."

"Dancing?"

"Yeah, pit dancing. I got bored. No one showed and then you disappeared. I was standing there like a tard holding that stupid sign and I just got crazy bored. So I started practicing my moves."

I made the mistake of asking, "What moves would those be?" At which point Tyler went into a frenetic gyration, twisting his body up, down and around as he wildly swung his arms and legs. This was in the parking lot, no doubt with security cameras rolling.

I yelled at him to stop, which was all I could do. Trying to grab him would have risked great physical harm.

"Floor punch!" he yelled.

"Tyler! Stop! That's enough!"

He explained that was how they danced at the rock shows he liked to go to. Something about ninja this and wall-of-death that. I didn't pretend to understand. I just told him if he wanted to hang around with me he'd have to refrain from doing any more of that.

I dropped Tyler off at Amber's school just in time to pick up his brother with the instructions that he should keep talking to Amber about the plot, keeping his finger on the pulse of where she was with this, and report back to me. She'd already confided in me about some crazy ideas. Who knew what she might tell Tyler?

12

I drove the Escalade to a motel and got a room. At the very least my home was under surveillance, so I thought it best to try to avoid it if I could. The next day I took a bus to the office. With everything going on I still had contacts to make, appointments to see, and paperwork to get done. Rich Fox asked what I'd been up to. I told him I was busy working leads in U.S. government agencies and the military. He left me alone after that, but I felt like I wasn't giving my job my full attention and it probably showed. Then at 5:45 I left for the Washington Monument.

I got down to 15th Street and started walking toward the monument. I didn't know whom I'd be looking for, but I had a feeling they would know me. As I got closer I still didn't see anybody. The monument was closed for repairs. But it was late and there were no workers around. At least I thought there weren't until two men in hard hats appeared and walked directly toward me.

They looked physically strong, as construction workers often do, but these two seemed different. Looking like cast members from World Wrestling Entertainment, they were huge and had odd features. One of them had a checkerboard design shaved into the sides of his head and the other wore pentagram-shaped earrings inside stretched lobes.

Checkers and pentagram approached and gently took my arm. Checkers said calmly, "Hello, sir. We'd like to have a word with you. Step this way, please."

They led me the few steps into the monument. But the moment the door closed their attitude changed dramatically. Pentagram grabbed me from behind while checkers got the elevator doors open. They pushed me in so hard I hit my face on the back wall.

"Hey! Wait!" I yelled. "What's going on? Whatever I did I can fix it!"

The two of them came in and closed the door. Checkers picked me up and pressed my face back against the wall. I could feel the elevator go up.

The observation floor of the Washington Monument is over 500 feet above the ground; it's like standing on the top floor of a 50-story building. On each of the four sides there are two rectangular windows for viewing the city. One hundred years ago it was fashionable for professional baseball players to attempt to catch balls thrown from one of those windows. By the time it reached the ground the ball would be traveling 100 mph. Most attempts to catch the balls were unsuccessful; a few succeeded, and one man received smashed teeth for his trouble.

The instant the doors opened, checkers rushed me out and pentagram pulled one of the observation windows out of its frame. Almost instantly they had me off the floor and moving toward the opened window.

There was a lot of flailing and struggling. "Shut up!" one of them yelled. They had me at the window and I kept wiggling my body and grabbing at things with my arms. "Did Ted Turdington send you?" I asked, but got no answer. I held onto them and tried to brace against the wall, but they were too strong and too good at their job. They had the upper half of my body out the window and kept knocking my hands off things I'd grabbed until there were no things left, just the bare outer wall of the Washington Monument. To say I was scared would be both inaccurate and an understatement. I was in an area beyond scared. I think I broke the fear barrier and passed into an entirely new realm of heightened apprehension.

I tried bending my knees and hooking my legs over the window sill, but my attackers had paused and were just holding on. "Do you know how easy it would be to drop you?" one of them said. I tried bending at the waist and raising myself up so I could grasp at the window with my hands, but as soon they saw me trying they lifted my calves and pushed me out the rest of the way. The über-fear rushed back. But again they didn't let go completely.

There I was, being held by my ankles upside-down out the top of the Washington Monument. The wind blew as I observed the horizon with, what I would have ordinarily considered, a beautiful sunset at the bottom and green grass and white buildings at the top. I gripped as best I could at the stone exterior of the monument, but it was designed to be smooth. Just below my head was a drop straight down of 500 feet.

The two of them shouted at me in rapid fire: "Do you want to die?!" "Drop him!" "I hate insurance salesmen!" "I'm gonna let go!" "Whoops!" "Make him eat the ground!" "Get rid of him; he knows too much!" "I'll give you a dollar to let go of him!" "Can you hear us? We hate you and we're going to kill you!" "There he goes!" "I can't hold on!" "He's slipping!" "Give us one good reason why we shouldn't drop you right now!"

"I can't hold on!"

"Not good enough!"

"I'll do anything you want!"

With that, they started pulling me back up. Finally I got inside the window, but before I had the chance to feel relieved checkers grabbed me and pushed me against the wall. "Did you mean it?"

"Mean what?"

"You'd do anything we say. Because if you don't, you won't see us coming next time. You won't have time to do shit. You'll be dead!"

"Yes, yes, yes."

"Stop what you're doing."

"Stop what?"

"Throw him back out!" yelled pentagram.

Checkers pulled me off the wall and the two of them started me toward the window. "Okay, okay, okay! I'll stop! I'll stop!"

"Stop what?" checkers asked.

"I'll stop looking for things I'm not supposed to."

"Why should we believe you?" pentagram shouted.

"Because I've had enough. I'm done."

They looked at each other, then checkers said, "Your every move is watched. We know what you're doing at all times. If you try anything, you're dead. Understand?"

"Yes, I do."

I looked down at the floor and noticed someone's BlackBerry lying there. I didn't own that brand, so I surmised it belonged to one of the two maniacs who'd assaulted me, probably popping out during the struggle. There was a map open on its screen, so I said to the two goons, "I dropped my BlackBerry."

I reached down and picked it up, and looked at it just long enough to see an address highlighted in Chevy Chase, Maryland. I cleared the screen and said, "Oh wait, this isn't mine."

Pentagram checked his pocket, said, "Give me that," and snatched it out of my hand.

As we went down the elevator it flashed through my mind that what I'd experienced was a hard-sell technique they don't teach in marketing school. I couldn't think of what situation might arise in my line of work that would give me the opportunity to use that one myself. It was obvious checkers and pentagram were selling something other than college-funding plans.

13

I didn't know if they'd been telling the truth, that my every move was being watched, but it didn't matter. I had to find Julia and I had to get to the bottom of this plot. That evening I took a cab and a bus and a train and a bus to the neighborhood on pentagram's BlackBerry.

Getting off at Chevy Chase Circle, I started down Grafton Street to the address shown on the map. This was a very nice neighborhood—large single family homes, all well maintained. I wondered what business those two goons had around here. I found the right number and looked around for a good approach. I wasn't sure going up to the front door would be a good idea. If this was ground zero for the assassination schemers they might not be too welcoming if I showed up. So under cover of darkness and the many trees in the area I snuck around back and peered in a window. There were lights on; it appeared someone was home. Looking out to not step on tree twigs, I carefully made my way around to another window. This one went to the kitchen, and inside, sure enough, I saw one of the pro wrestlers from the Washington Monument—pentagram. He got something out of the refrigerator and took a swig off it—probably some illegal growth hormone, I thought.

He left the room, and I went around to the other side of the house where I found a tree that would give me a good view of the second floor, if I could climb it. I grasped hold of a small branch and pulled myself up, but quickly realized this was a mistake as the branch snapped from my weight and I fell with a thud to the ground. I looked up at the house to see if the noise had generated any activity. I thought I was safe, but a dog had started barking. The sound seemed close enough that it could be coming from this property, but I wasn't sure. Eventually, the barking stopped and I got back up and tried again.

This time I made sure to grab only large branches and, trying to keep rustling to a minimum, I slowly ascended high enough to see inside the second floor windows. Then, pay dirt! As I peered into a second-floor bedroom I caught the unmistakable silhouette of Julia's head. She was seated with her back to me, but I knew her hair style and the shape of her body. It was Julia, alright. And she appeared to be alone.

Then out of the corner of my eye I caught movement in another window. A man was walking around in another room. I strained to see his face. He seemed familiar. Then it hit me. It was my "host" from the Secret Service. Nine Grafton Street in Chevy Chase, Maryland, certainly was shaping up to be the malevolent vortex of a plot to overthrow the democratically elected government of the United States. I had to do something. I had to get Julia out of there.

I climbed out of the tree and went toward where I'd heard the dog barking. It was actually in the next-door neighbor's yard. Having seen an open window on the first floor of the house I'd been casing, I got an idea. If I climbed in that window chances were

I wouldn't get far with pentagram, "host," and who knows who else in there. But if I created a diversion, I'd have half a chance.

I went around to the neighbor's yard. The dog was a golden retriever and seemed very friendly. I unhooked him from his chain and led him around to the house imprisoning Julia. Then with one big hoist I lifted the dog to the open window and let him stumble on in. He reacted perfectly, running around frantically, knocking things off tables, and generally disturbing everything. I heard someone yell, then I saw pentagram chasing the dog from room to room. Finally, he walked through holding the dog's collar as both he and my "host" led him toward the front door. The second I heard the front door latch I climbed in the window myself. I quickly found a staircase leading up, and went to the room Julia was in.

"Hank! What are you doing here?"

"Shhh! We have to get you out of here."

Julia was restrained by an ankle shackle connected to a long cable. The room had a private bath and the cable was long enough for her to reach all necessary areas—her kidnappers had thought of everything. The problem was how to get her disconnected from the cable? While pondering this I took a quick peek downstairs. Pentagram and "host" were back inside, but were busy cleaning and straightening things up.

I came back to Julia's room and, as I looked for some way to get her free, asked her what these guys had been doing to her.

"Nothing," she said. "That big guy down there and a friend of his took me when I got home from work."

"Checkers," I said.

"What?"

"The other one has a haircut like a checker board, right?"

"Yeah. How did you know?"

"Let's just say I'm familiar with those two. The other one's not here is he?"

"No, just the one. Plus that guy in the suit."

"So they haven't hurt you?"

"No, not at all. Except for this ankle thing, they've been very nice. You know, they might be criminals and kidnappers, but I think you would like them. Maybe you could set up their retirement accounts."

"Very funny, Julia. Have they told you what any of this is about?"

"No. They're careful not to say much around me. But I did overhear something when they were out in the hall."

As I looked around for anything that could be used to cut the cable, I castigated myself for not thinking of bringing tools with me.

"Hank, I've already looked everywhere at least three times."

"So, what did you hear them talking about?"

"They kept saying something about this guy who works at the Smithsonian. They kept calling him 'Tousand.'"

"Thousand?"

"No, Tousand. Like thousand without the 'h'. I heard them mention the National Air and Space Museum, so I guess that's where he is."

"Why were they talking about him?"

"I didn't hear very much. I got the name because they kept repeating it over and over. Whatever it was, they were taking this guy pretty seriously."

The other end of Julia's cable was padlocked around the base of the toilet. Deciding this to be the weakest link, I went to work on the toilet. Suddenly, I heard Julia shriek, "Hank!" I don't remember what happened next. However, it must have involved my head falling into the toilet because when I woke up my hair was all wet.

I was back on the first floor sitting on a sofa across from my "host." I lifted my arm and found the other arm following it. My wrists had been handcuffed.

"I like you, Mr. Stafford. That's why I put the handcuffs on in front instead of the back."

"Thanks. That's very considerate of you, Mr.... What was your name again?"

There were two empty glasses and a pitcher of water on the table. My "host" poured water into both glasses, then drank from his.

"Fresh, cold water," he said. "Drink it. It'll clear your head."

I took a sip off of mine and listened as he spoke.

"The United States won World War I, and we won World War II. You can see the memorial to that effort out on the Mall."

"I just saw it upside down yesterday. Not many people get a chance to do that. I feel blessed."

"After a more than 40-year struggle, Mr. Stafford, we prevailed in the Cold War. Now America's enemies have become even more clever, more insidious, and less constrained by morals and common decency than ever. After over a century of advancing America's position in the world, we can't let our guard down now and allow all those hard-fought gains to be chipped away. If you go to Arlington National Cemetery you'll be surrounded by symbols of the blood that has been spilled advancing us to the pinnacle that we now occupy."

"I've been there. It's a nice place."

"Mr. Stafford, we are the dominant nation on earth. But being in a position like that brings responsibility. None of our national leaders may avoid that responsibility, or pretend that there are no costs associated with shepherding that responsibility. To downplay that central aspect of our position in the world will only encourage challenges to our vital interests. We have to continue to lead and expand our influence, and not just react to what others are doing. We have to do whatever is necessary to ensure that the United States remains, far into the future, the preeminent power in the world. We have to avoid, at all costs, allowing our advantage to slip away. The security of the world must continue to depend upon a fully engaged and motivated United States of America. To ignore that calling would be a tragedy of historic proportions. The continued peace and prosperity of the rest of the world depend on the benevolent protection provided by the United States. And we can't allow the vagaries of our electoral process to darken the purity of our global leadership."

"When are you planning on killing President Obama?"

"I don't know what you're talking about, Mr. Stafford. Our operations haven't uncovered any threat against the president. He is in the safest, most secure hands he could possibly be in. The question is what are your intentions?"

"My intention is to free Julia, stop you from killing President Obama, expose you to the world, and then maybe sell you a long-term-care insurance policy with an inflation-adjustment rider."

He laughed. "Mr. Stafford, I have enjoyed our time together, but I have to go now." With that, my "host" got up, gestured to pentagram, and the two of them went through the house knocking things over and pulling handfuls of items out of drawers, scattering them around the floor.

"You guys just cleaned up," I said. "What are you doing?" But my head felt like an echo chamber as I said it. Extreme dizziness began to set in. I thought the water was safe because my "host" had also drunk it, but there must have been something in my glass not visible to the naked eye that mixed with the water after it was poured in. When I went to brush something off my shoulder and it turned out to be the floor, I knew I was in trouble.

"Host" removed my handcuffs as pentagram brought Julia downstairs. Now nearly paralyzed, I watched helplessly as they took her out the back door. Struggling to remain conscious, I remembered seeing chunked chocolate in a bowl on the coffee table. Using all my strength to reach up and slide the bowl onto the floor, I chewed on the chocolate as best I could. Eventually feeling a slight energy boost, I managed to wiggle myself along the floor and then tried to stand up. But as soon as I got my head more than two feet off the ground I completely lost all sense of balance and toppled over. So I crawled to the front door and tried getting up again. The chocolate seemed to be kicking in more by now and I could get up to my knees and unlock the door. Holding onto the door knob and leaning against the jamb I got up on my feet and moved outside. I'd often used bulk dark chocolate to help get me through that fourth interview appointment of the day and it seemed to be doing the trick now when I needed it most.

Keeping my feet wide and my arms outstretched I kept my balance as I slowly made it to the sidewalk. There I started toward Chevy Chase Circle. Like a pilot who's lost all his instrumentation and can't trust his senses, I used my vision to decide how to stay upright. If the tops of the trees started coming into view I adjusted forward. If I saw the ground tilting left or right I adjusted accordingly. Just as I was reaching the circle three police cars sped around it and went into Grafton Street. I could only guess they were going to the house I'd just left—their sounds seemed to terminate there. But I didn't dare turn around to look as I surely would not have remained upright following such a maneuver. I got to the bus stop and sat, eating the chocolate I'd stuffed into my pockets as I waited. When the bus came I got on it and became just another Saturday-night drunk out on the town.

14

Having spent the rest of the weekend sleeping off the effects of whatever it was they'd given me, on Monday morning I called the National Air and Space Museum and asked for "Mr. Tousand," not really expecting to get very far. But a few seconds after my initial inquiry, a man came on the phone and said, "Hello, how can I help you?"

"Um, hi. Is this Mr. Tousand?"

"Yes. Who am I speaking with?"

"Oh, hello, Mr. Tousand. My name's Hank Stafford with National American Life of Maryland. How are you today?"

I heard a sigh at the other end. "Listen, Hank, I'm very busy and I just can't talk right now."

"I understand you're busy, Mr. Tousand. But a friend of yours who I've done some business with said I should give you a call, that you might be interested in hearing what I have to say."

"Oh? Which friend?"

"He works for the National Threat Assessment Center at the Secret Service."

There was a long pause. Finally I said, "Mr. Tousand, are

you still there?"

"Meet me out on the Mall at noon. Go straight out from the museum. I'll be at the first crosswalk." Then the line disconnected.

I stood at the designated crosswalk at the appointed time and waited. After a short time I saw a man rise from a nearby bench and walk toward me. He was a neat, nerdy-looking fellow in his 50s. "Are you here waiting for someone?" he said.

"Yes. You must be Mr. Tousand."

"Tell me your name again."

"Hank Stafford. Nice to meet you." I went to shake his hand. He didn't respond.

"Do you have any identification?"

"Yes," I said and gave him my card.

"A life insurance salesman," Tousand said with a chuckle. "That's almost too creative for them. I almost believe you."

"I prefer 'financial services professional'. I help people with much more than just life insurance. You see, there's a whole range of...."

"How do you know the man from the Secret Service?" he said, cutting me off.

"I meet a lot of people in my line of work. I think we met at a social event or...."

"Okay, okay. Serves me right for asking. Now listen, go to Epiphany Catholic Church in Georgetown tomorrow morning for their regular service. Sit in the last pew on the right, all the way to the right. We'll continue this conversation at that time." Tousand turned the moment he'd finished talking and walked back to the museum.

I spent the rest of the day trying to catch up on some actual business-related appointments. My work had been suffering since this whole thing started and I had to try to maintain at least some semblance of my normal operation, not just because Rich Fox would begin wondering what was up—I'd been one of the most consistent agents in the office—but because my own income depended on it. If I couldn't get signatures on at least two new applications every week I might as well have found a new job. My only thought as I sat visiting with Mr. and Mrs. Norbert Graham of Waterloo, Maryland, was the hope they wouldn't now be on some evil organization's hit list as a result of their agreeing to meet with me. Dead customers cannot be repeat customers.

The next morning I went to Epiphany Catholic Church as directed and sat waiting in the last pew for Tousand to show up. Then I waited and waited some more. The service was moving along, opening comments were made, hymns were sung. It was nearly time for communion and I was growing impatient. I hadn't looked at the Bible or hymnal resting at my location, but boredom now compelled me to pick them up. As I lifted the Bible I noticed a slip of paper sticking out near the back. I opened it to the Book of Revelations and saw something written on the piece of paper. The note read: "My coming has been delayed. Keep the faith. I will contact you."

I looked up and suddenly saw checkers standing at the side door. Turning to the left, there was pentagram at the front door. Startled, I closed the book with a thud, causing two congregants to turn to see where the noise was coming from. I decided to stay put for the time being. As long as I was inside this church with all these people I was relatively safe. But what would happen once the service ended? An old priest performed the ritual prior to communion and everyone—except me, checkers and pentagram— went up to receive it. Then the priest gave his sermon and I began to build a mild panic. I had to think of some way to get out of there alive.

The sermon for the day centered on the story of Joseph in the Book of Genesis. The old priest began with some back story and then said, "And that's when Jacob gave to his son a wonderful coat of diverse colors...."

"Wait a minute!" I shouted, and ran around the pews to keep as far away from pentagram and checkers as possible. Going to the front I said, "Just a minute, just a minute. Now excuse me, folks. I'm sorry, I'm new here. I just want to get one thing straight."

"Then sit down," someone called from the pews.

"Oh I will. But I was just wondering, father, why you referred to it as a 'coat of diverse colors.'"

"Son," the old priest replied. "I'm getting to that in my sermon. Will you please be patient and be seated?"

"No, no, no, no. Sorry, but your referring to it as a 'coat of diverse colors' is incorrect. That translation was debunked years ago."

"Yes, you're right. I'm sorry, it's a really a long tunic. Now will you please sit so I can continue?"

I looked around at the two malevolent doorkeepers. They appeared a bit nervous, but were holding their ground. "Whoa, whoa, whoa," I continued. "I think if we're supposed to trust you to deliver the word of God as spoken through the Bible, then you should get it right."

A woman from the pews shouted, "Who do you think you are? Sit down and be quiet."

"Ma'am, I'll tell you. I'm an expert on the Bible. I used to sell Bible software for a company out in Iowa and I know all about it."

"Are you crazy?" someone asked. "Will you please let Father Tim continue?"

"Listen, I sold all the versions of the Bible: King James, New International, Revised Standard, New Revised Standard, New Jerusalem Bible, the New American Bible, which is the version you folks use these days. And in that one it sure doesn't say Joseph got a coat of diverse colors. I bet I could tell the story better than him."

"Alright, son," the priest said. "Sit down and I promise to get everything right from now on."

I looked around again. "No, no, no. You don't get off that easy. How do we know you won't get something really big wrong? Like saying Abraham's son had it coming or something like that."

At this point some of the men of the congregation got up and started moving my way. I thought getting thrown out by them would help me get past the two stooges, but then what would happen once I got outside? No, I needed more help.

"I bet this guy is a closet Baptist. I bet he reads the King James Version when he's alone and thinks no one is looking."

Two men came by my side. "Please, sir, come with us," one of them said.

"What are you gonna do if I don't?"

"Nothing. We don't want any trouble. We don't want to call the police."

I stepped away from them. "Well I think you should," I said. I'd thought about calling the police myself, but having them just show up wasn't enough. I needed them to take me away from there. "Did you know there was a break-in at a house in Chevy Chase on Saturday? Do you know who did it? The police must be called. In fact, if you don't call the police right now, I'm going to stay here and tell you all about how Father Tim has been drilling for oil in altar boys for the last 40 years!"

Several hands began dialing 911 at once. When the police arrived, I was outside surrounded by a group of congregants, while pentagram and checkers looked on from the side. The good folks explained to the police what I'd been doing and my claim that I'd broken into a house in Chevy Chase. So the cops took me into custody.

Sitting in the back of the cruiser I felt that, as good as it was to be escorted away from there by armed officials, being thrown in jail for B&E would be bad for business. So I thought I'd take a chance and tell them the truth, partially. "I didn't really break into that house," I said. "The people living there kidnapped my friend, and I went there to try to get her out. I didn't break in. I climbed in through an opened window. And I didn't mess the place up. Those guys drugged me and then wrecked the place to try to make it look like I was a burglar."

They weren't buying it. But I gave them Julia's name and one of them said, "Oh, that's Peggy Scheider's daughter."

"You know Peggy?"

"The whole department knows Peggy by now. She's practically living down at headquarters."

"So you know I'm telling the truth. Her daughter Julia was kidnapped."

"We don't have any evidence of that. We're not investigating that case."

"But I'm giving you the evidence right now. Go to that house in Chevy Chase and talk to the people that live there."

The cops actually took the suggestion and we rode up to Chevy Chase. Stopping in front of the house, they left me handcuffed in the back seat while they went up to the front door and knocked. I could see what was going on from my vantage point and someone answered the door. But it wasn't my "host" or pentagram or anyone like that. "Holy shit, is that George Will?"

I watched with my jaw hanging open as the two police

officers stood at the front door of the house where I'd been drugged and my friend held prisoner having a conversation with columnist and TV talk-show commentator George F. Will. I couldn't believe it. I'd watched him on "This Week with George Stephanopoulos" and never imagined that he could be a central figure in a coup d'tat against the United States government. He seemed like such a nice fellow, so nice that he was even a Chicago Cubs baseball fan. But maybe it was all a cover. My mind began to race as the cops finished talking to Mr. Will and returned to the cruiser.

"Was that George Will?" I asked as they got back in.

"Listen to me," one of them said. "The owner of the house was out of town with his family for the past week. They just got back yesterday. He says nothing was taken or seriously damaged and he doesn't want to press charges. You should consider yourself extremely lucky."

"But...."

"Let me finish. You may not be going to jail today, but we've got your information, which we are sharing with the Chevy Chase Police Department. If you are seen anywhere in this neighborhood, you will be picked up. Do you understand?"

I thought about asking what if I had an insurance appointment up there? After all, this was a fairly well-off demographic and I'd hate to have to cut it out of my territory—a few estate-planning cases alone could push me into MDRT status. But I figured I'd better let sleeping dogs lie, for now. "Yeah, I understand."

I rode back into DC pondering the likelihoods that George Will was either a victim of these people same as I was or an evil mastermind bent on destroying democracy as we knew it. The jury remained out on that one as the cops dropped me off at DuPont

Circle.

15

Later my TracFone rang and it was Amber. She said she missed me and really wanted to see me and that she had something important she wanted to discuss with me. After finding out she was calling from a pay phone I gave her directions to my motel room. When she dropped by late that afternoon, I went to kiss her but she pulled back.

"Not yet," she said. "I can't wait any longer."

I was confused. "Can't wait?"

"For Todd. He's coming home on Friday. He'll be there Friday and Saturday, and then he's going back to Fort Myer Saturday evening. He doesn't know when he'll be back after that."

"Well, that will be nice to spend some time with him, won't it?"

Amber looked at me like I was mentally defective. "Hank, I can't wait. I've got it all planned out."

"What have you got planned out, Amber?"

"I know how I'm going to get rid of Todd."

I turned and walked away. "Okay, I'm pretty sure I really don't want to be hearing this."

"I'm going to use antifreeze."

"Amber, maybe you should go now."

"I can't go, Hank. I thought you loved me."

"Maybe I do. So, as somebody who loves you, I'm telling you this is not a good idea. And anyway what about Todd's mission?" Until now, Amber's talk of doing something to Todd had all been very abstract, and if anything were to be done it would be Amber alone. I would wake up one morning, get a call that Todd had died, act surprised, and go from there. But now Amber was here with me in a motel room talking about love and wanting to divulge to me all of the details of how and when she was planning to kill her husband. Having prior knowledge of a crime that might be committed was bad enough, but becoming a full accomplice was a position I had no desire to be in.

Not to mention, there was reason to believe the attempt on President Obama's life would take place on Memorial Day, this coming Monday. Amber was not aware of that; neither I nor Tyler had told her. So if she went through with her plan, she would be killing a person who was directly involved in the plot two days before it hatched.

But was it really to take place on Memorial Day? And which side was Todd on? Was he an integral member of the team that would thwart the assassins? Or was he the assassin himself? Letting Amber go through with her plan would either give the assassination a chance to succeed or it would be like killing John Wilkes Booth two days before Lincoln went to Ford's Theatre. I didn't know which it was.

Amber continued talking while all this was going through my head, and most of what she said did not register. But when she put her arm around my neck and her other hand on my crotch, I snapped back to the here and now. She gave me a deep kiss, pushed me down onto the bed, and got on top of me, straddling my body as she unbuttoned various articles of clothing, both mine and hers. We remained in that position, Amber on top, and we went at it—forgetting for the moment about her husband and the plotters.

Afterward, as she lay down on top of me, her naked body pressing into mine, we engaged in some unusual pillow talk. "Antifreeze poisoning can look like a heart attack," she said.

"A heart attack? Todd's healthy as a horse. They're going to know something's wrong."

"No, because Todd has a heart condition already."

"Even worse. If it looks like he died of a previous heart condition that he had knowledge of, then the company won't pay because he knowingly misrepresented that fact on his insurance application."

"What if he didn't know?"

"How could he not know? You know about it. How did you find out?"

"From his mother. She told me when we became engaged that Todd was born with a hole in his valve or something. It's serious. He could die sometime soon anyway. But the suspense is killing me. I just want it to be over."

I shook my head. "If that were true, his doctors would have a record. It would have come up in one of his exams. His Army exam, for example. And how come he doesn't know?"

She shook her head back at me. "Because his mother didn't want him to know. She didn't want him to limit himself in life. She wanted him to lead as full a life as he could without this thing holding him back. She never told him. She switched from the original doctor who found it and never had his medical records forwarded. It takes a special test to find it. A stress test or something."

"That must be why our doctor didn't find it. We only do EKGs, not stress tests."

"Then you think it's a good idea?"

"No," I said, trying as much to convince myself as Amber. "There's just too much that can go wrong. The smallest suspicion could lead them to perform the test that would find antifreeze and bring the whole thing crashing down. It's not worth it. Unless...."

"Unless what?"

"I have to find out more, Amber." I rolled her off of me. "Whatever you do it's okay with me. Um, I just don't want to know any more about it." I started to get dressed. "But I might have to call you and tell you not to do it, or at least to wait. Can you do that?"

"No, Hank. It's all planned for Friday. He works out every day. I'm going to put the antifreeze in his Gatorade. I don't know when he'll be back home again."

I went up to her and held her arms. "Amber, please. If I have to tell you to wait there's a really good reason for it."

"What reason?"

"Amber, do you care if the president of the United States is going to be assassinated?"

"Hank, I've been thinking about that and I can't count on it. I told you I wasn't a risk taker, and that's not a sure thing. What if nothing happens? The way I'm doing it is a much better bet."

"A risk taker? What you're planning to do is the biggest risk there is."

"Can I ask you a question?"

"Sure."

"Do you care about one million dollars?"

I made yet another fatal hesitation. Asking me if I cared about $1,000,000 was one of those is-the-Pope-Catholic questions.

"Yes," I said finally. "But I'll have a hard time spending it if I'm in prison for the rest of my life." I said this even as I began pondering how $1,000,000 in life insurance proceeds could be successfully laundered. Just as a hypothetical exercise, of course.

"Do you trust me?" Amber asked.

Another hesitation. "Let me say I would feel better about it if you would wait if I tell you to."

Amber walked up to me, lifted her head, and kissed me slowly and deeply. Pulling back, she said, "Don't worry, honey. Everything is going to be alright."

Amber left my motel room, but left me pondering another possibility: Was I being set up? I seemed to be getting inextricably involved in a murder/insurance-fraud scheme, without ever having agreed to anything. The appearance of impropriety was going to start looking like the picture of Dorian Gray real soon. Maybe if I could get to the bottom of the assassination plot by Friday, and find out exactly what Todd's role in it was, I could have the proper authorities get to him before his wife did.

I called the office to check my voicemail messages and who should be on there but Susan Underhill, the woman from the airport. Susan said she wanted to see me right away about getting my input on a taco business she was opening. "That's right, you heard me," she said. I called her back and asked her why she had to see me right now. She told me she was about to close the deal and she wanted to show it to me first. I wanted to try to contact Mr. Tousand of the Smithsonian again, but on the off chance that Susan really had potential business for me, I took the bait. I thought it would be safe to give her my motel and room number, and within an hour she was there.

She strode in the door saying, "Mr. Henry A. 'Hank'

Stafford, I knew the first time I saw you, I wanted you advising me."

Well, it turned out that Susan wasn't really opening a taco business. I knew she was coming on to me at the airport, and that she was coming on to me here as well. Maybe it's a character defect, but I was the type of person who felt if someone else wanted to pursue some activity, who was I to tell them no? Live and let live. I had my own things I needed to concentrate on; let people do what they wanted as long as it didn't interfere with my own business. Of course, this approach was easy to stick to when it involved women throwing themselves at me. Still, some amount of caution might have been advised since one is not always sure just what the motives are of the other.

And I did have something important I needed to be working on. But she stood close to me giving me that look that said "If you don't kiss me now, you're going to feel like an idiot within an hour after I leave." So I did, and we made out for a long time. Having just had sex, I took my time and went slower with Susan. I went down on her; discouraged her from going down on me. And when I lamented the fact I didn't have any rubbers with me, she produced her own. Susan was very physical in bed, at one point digging her nails into my back so hard I felt she must have drawn blood.

When we were done she said she had to get back to see her mother, but that she really enjoyed my company and wanted to see me again. She asked for my cell phone number, and I gave it to her. As Susan left I pondered the fact that no matter what happened with this assassination plot, it was getting me the most action I'd seen in a long time.

16

I knew the note Mr. Tousand had left said he would contact me, but I felt I had no time to wait and I took the initiative. The next morning, I had my phone in my hand preparing to call him when the phone rang first. And like before, it was not a number I recognized. "Great," I thought. "The TracFone company is going to get rich off of me."

"Hello, Mr. Stafford?"

"Who's this?" I didn't recognize the voice.

"This is a friend. I know where they took Julia."

"Where? Tell me."

"They took her to Hunting Hill Quarry. It's on Piney Meetinghouse Road in Rockville."

"Okay, got it. Now who is this?"

"I can't tell you. I'm afraid for my life. I just want to help."

"How did you get this number?" But the call disconnected before I could finish the question.

Somehow the TracFone had been compromised again, so I used the pay phone down the street to call the Air and Space Museum. And for the second time I got right through to Mr.

Tousand. If it were as easy to get through to the person who could help you at most businesses as it was to get through to a person with knowledge of a plot to assassinate the president, then we'd be in great shape in this country. Once Tousand found out I was calling from a pay phone, he told me to come see him Thursday at noon at the museum, but to be sure not to use my real name.

I made a note of the appointment in my mental planner, then got in the rented Escalade and pointed it toward Rockville. The Hunting Hill Quarry was about a half-hour away, giving me time to think about how to approach the kidnappers if I should run into them, and also how I might be able to claim this Escalade, the motel room and the TracFones as business expenses on my next tax return.

I turned off Piney Meetinghouse Road and started down a paved, well-kept road into the quarry. There were a group of buildings and parked vehicles ahead. I stopped there, taking this to be the quarry offices. Carefully I surveyed the area as I walked up to the first building. I was not familiar with what quarries normally looked like when they weren't being used as evil lairs for kidnapper/assassins, but everything seemed alright so far. I went into the office and saw a man at the counter. I didn't recognize him. He wore a uniform with a patch over one shirt pocket that said "Hunting Hill Quarry" and a patch over the other that said "Jim." So I assumed he worked there. "Hello, sir," I said to him.

"'Lo, wut kyin ah do fer yeu."

Here I breathed a sigh of relief, because unless the CIA was recruiting Baltimore city goats for their black ops, I was safe with this guy. "This may be an odd question," I said, "but have you seen any unusual people come in here this morning?"

"Unyuzhl? Wut kahna peepl ya lookin fer?"

"They would probably be a couple of guys with a woman.

At least one of the guys would be huge, built like a pro wrestler."

"Raysslin? We don git no raysslers rahn here."

"I don't think he's really a wrestler. The point is...."

"Yeu tha caps?"

"Actually, I'm a private investigator. There's been a kidnapping, and we have reason to believe the perpetrators may be trying to use this quarry as a hiding place."

"Hahdina kwahree? They gotta be nuts. Sall open space. Ain't no playssa hahdahn thayer."

"Would you mind if I took a look around."

"S awite. I dun do tha harn n farn rahn here. Boss won be in t tuhmar."

"So it's okay with you?"

"Wud I jessay? Jess dun gestuk inna sawl."

So I went and looked around in the other buildings. There weren't many workers there. It seemed to be a slow day; not much going on. The buildings looked clear, and I thought if I were a kidnapper I might try going farther down into the quarry to avoid detection. I got back in the Escalade and drove down the dirt road used by the quarry trucks. Hunting Hill Quarry was almost three quarters of a mile long and over a quarter mile wide, so there was lots of ground to cover. I drove about as far in as I could, near the deepest part, and still hadn't seen any unusual activity. I stopped for a moment to plan my next move.

Getting out of the SUV, I stood next to it surveying the landscape. The guy at the counter was right: lots of open space, not a great place to hide—except the area was so large that something could happen at one end and the people at the other end would never know about it. Just then I heard a noise, the sound of a very large machine. But the noise grew louder and closer by the second. I looked through the windows of the Escalade and saw one of those enormous mining trucks coming straight at me at around 40 miles per hour. I bolted perpendicular to its direction and kept running. With my back turned I heard a tremendous crash. Thinking the thing must have wrecked itself, I turned and saw a stunning sight. My rented Cadillac Escalade was completely flat. The mining truck had run over one of the biggest SUVs on the market and rendered it the height of a kiddie pool. The truck, meanwhile, didn't appear to have a scratch on it and was now in the process of turning toward me.

This thing was huge. Over 20 feet high, it was like a rolling two-story building. It was almost 50 feet long and nearly 30 feet wide, the tires alone on this thing were over 12 feet high. It easily weighed several hundred tons. I'd already seen its speed; I could never outrun it. And now it was drawing a bead on me. I heard it's gears shift and its engine rev. So I ran. But where to run to? The surface of this quarry consisted of essentially two angles: 0 degrees and 90 degrees, flat open ground and walls of rock going straight up. I tried running a zig zag pattern, but whoever was driving the thing knew what he was doing and stayed right with me. I jumped out from in front of a giant tire just before it touched me, and I tried running around to the back. But it made a quick turn and gave chase again.

This time I ran straight toward one of the rock walls. The truck was so big, there was about three feet of clearance between the ground its bottom. I thought if I could get under there without getting clipped by a tire, I could use that to my advantage. Sure enough, I got to the rock wall and stopped, ducking to the ground right before the truck smashed into the wall right over my head. But I was safe and got out along the side just before the driver put it in reverse and backed up, the tire rolling over where I'd just been a split second before.

I'd hoped the driver would be dazed or think I'd been crushed, and I'd be able to sneak off. But he quickly backed it way up and, seeing me, the chase was on once more. I ran out into the open area, stopped and ducked into the truck's three-foot clearance as it passed all the way over me. I ran away, he turned, and gave chase again. I ducked again, but he was starting to get wise and turned sharply just as I went under. I had to roll away to keep the back tire from crushing me.

This game of cat and mouse seemed to go on forever. I kept looking for ways to escape or ways to disable the beast, but to no avail. I could never get enough of a head start to make it back to civilization, and this driver was so agile with this thing that every time I tried grabbing hold of it, he'd have it moving again and I risked falling and getting run over. I was breathing very heavily by this point. My running speed was slowing and it was growing more difficult to make sharp evasive maneuvers. He was wearing me down and he must have known it.

Then I got to a vantage point where I could see farther down into the quarry. There was another level accessible by road, but with those 90 degree drops all around it. I got up one more time and ran toward a drop, then ran parallel to it at first, about 20 feet away. I waited until the truck was almost upon me and then made a sudden turn toward the drop. The driver took the bait. He swerved toward me thinking he was going in for the kill. I hit the ground. The truck passed over me, but its wheel went over the edge, dropping the clearance at that point to zero. I was tucked slightly farther in and the bottom of the truck came to within six inches of my head. Then it started to slide and twist. Clearance was getting worse and tires were coming toward me. I made my best guess where I might miss getting hit and then closed my eyes. I heard a crash, and when I opened my eyes there was no longer a giant mining truck hanging over me.

I looked over the edge and saw it on its side down at the bottom of the lowest level in the quarry. I didn't know who had been driving it—though I had a good guess—and I watched for any activity. Seeing none, I decided whoever had been driving was either dead or unconscious—though I wasn't eager to get close enough to verify that theory. I'd just been chased by a multi-hundred-ton truck; I had no desire to now be chased by an enraged killer undoubtedly carrying firearms. I walked back up to the quarry offices, past my squished Cadillac Escalade, thinking how I'd been penny wise but pound foolish when I'd declined the extra insurance coverage in the rental contract.

Back at the office, the same fellow was there and looked me over. When I'd last seen him just under an hour earlier I'd been neat, tidy, and clean. Now my clothes were filthy and ripped, and I had bruises and small cuts all over my body.

"Whoo, hon. Wud yu git inteeu?"

"There's been an accident."

"Ain't no ayxiden. Sa kuhtaystruffy. Yu look layu bun uzzaza ripper tahn on wonna r frun loder buks."

"Sir, I'm sorry. I'm not sure what you just said. But I think there may be a person injured down there who may need medical assistance." Still a bit dazed, I started to make my way out, but thought I'd mention one more thing. "Oh, there's also a crushed Cadillac SUV down there, but don't worry about that. It's a rental."

The Plot To Assassinate Barack Obama

17

I proceeded to lose myself in the Washington metro-area transit system, getting on a bus on Piney Meetinghouse Road, then switching to another bus, getting on the train at the Rockville station, riding a few different lines, then getting on another bus or two, and finally starting the half-mile walk back to the motel. Even after all that, I was two blocks into the walking portion of my trip when I heard a familiar seething sound behind me. I turned to see Ted Turdington scowling at me.

"Oh, it's you," I said with equal parts relief and trepidation.

"Yeah, it's me," Turdington shouted. "You're about to spend the rest of your life in prison. You should think about being more polite."

"I'm sorry if I'm not happy to see you, Special Agent Turdington. I had kind of a rough morning."

"I can see that. So are you going to tell me what happened, or are you going to sit on that too and maybe have it added to your jail sentence?"

"Why do you keep saying I'm going to jail? What have I done?"

"Conspiracy to commit murder," Turdington bellowed. "That ring a bell?"

"No, it doesn't. I don't know what you're talking about."

Turdington let out the longest sigh I'd ever heard, then said, "Okay, tell me you don't know a person by the name of Amber Manderville. Please tell me that, so you don't disappoint expectations, so you're still batting a thousand in dumb decisions."

"Yeah, I know Amber Manderville."

"That's good. Perfect. Beautiful. Now, keep in that same mode. Keep thinking to yourself 'If I were actually going to tell the truth, what would I say?' And tell me why you and Amber Manderville are planning to kill her husband."

I thought to myself "Oh, shit."

"Yeah, 'Oh, shit,'" Turdington said, reading my mind. "Now let's say, for the sake of argument, that you don't actually want to go on death row. And knowing that the first step in achieving that goal is to tell Special Agent Turdington everything you know about this plan to kill Todd Manderville, what are you going to do, Hank?"

I had to think for a second. No matter how you sliced it, this wasn't going well. If Ted Turdington was a real FBI agent, then Amber's plan was already getting me ensnared in serious legal trouble. If Turdington was a fake, he still knew about Amber's plan and would be using it in some sort of blackmail attempt—at the very least.

"What kind of deal can you get me if I tell you everything?"

Turdington exploded. "You want a deal?! You haven't told me shit. You haven't given me anything, and already you want a deal?"

"Yeah, I think that's reasonable. What if I start cooperating and there's really no chance of getting a deal after all."

"Do I look like Monty Hall? I must look like Monty fucking

Hall. Alright, I'm Monty Hall. And I can see you came here today dressed like an asshole. Well, Hank, there are just two boxes to choose from. If you continue to be an asshole, there's no choice. You get box number one. I'll even tell you what's in box number one. It's not a lifetime supply of tuna; it's a needle filled with a lifetime supply of death. Now, if you cooperate fully, you get what's in box number two. What's in box number two? The possibility that it's not box number one! Understand? Or is there a Monty Hall problem here?"

"I think I understand, but I just need time to think about it."

"You need time to think? I can tell you if I were presented with a choice like that I wouldn't have to think long, maybe a nanosecond."

"I want to do the right thing. I just have to take a little time, that's all."

"Alright, alright, alright. Let me cut to the chase. Correct me if I'm wrong, but this was all Amber's idea wasn't it? She initiated the idea; she planned it; she wants to carry it out. She just brought you in to facilitate the life insurance part and for general support. Am I pretty close so far?"

"Um, that sounds close."

"Good. So what I need from you is to help us stop Amber from killing Todd and help us get enough evidence on her to lock her up for a very long time. If you do that, there's a good chance you get off light."

Here I'm thinking this guy originally accosted me because he said I was some kind of terrorist. Now he knows about Amber's plan to kill Todd, and he's very eager to prevent that from happening. I was beginning to think Tyler was right about both Turdington and Todd. It just fit too perfectly. When I began investigating the assassination plot against the president, Turdington showed up and tried to scare me off of that. Now, with the possibility Todd may be killed before the attempt on President Obama, Turdington shows up again, doing everything he can to prevent that from happening.

"So do you still think I'm a terrorist?" I asked.

"Yes. But you've been wrangled and tamed, Mr. Al Qaeda in America."

"So what does my relationship with Amber Manderville have to do with that?"

Turdington got in my face and screamed, "Do you think I'm a pinhead?! You playing me for a shitheel?! I have a one hundred fifty-five IQ! I play the French horn! If you think you can win a game of mental chess with me you are wrong!"

"Okay. I'm sorry I asked."

"I'm an excruciatingly patient person, Hank. But this is beginning to bore the shit out of me. I need an answer from you right now. Are you going to help us crucify Amber Manderville or are you two going to flip to see who gets strapped onto the death table first?"

My relationship with Amber was such that I had no intention of protecting her out of principle. If lightning was going to strike her I didn't want to be standing nearby. But on the other hand, we'd grown close in our own weird way. And I really didn't like the way Turdington was talking about her. Even more importantly, she would be changing the course of history if she went through with her scheme. But as yet I didn't know whether that change would be for good or bad. Would she be indirectly saving President Obama's life or allowing him to die? And not knowing whether Ted Turdington was with the good guys or bad, I couldn't trust him. My only choice was to keep stalling until I could find out more. So I fainted.

I crumpled to the ground, even letting my head bump the sidewalk pretty hard to make it look real. Then I lay there in a twisted heap.

"What is this?" Turdington yelled. But I didn't move. I just made a little gurgling sound. I heard him pause for a few seconds before he leaned down and slipped something into my shirt collar. Then he said in relatively calm, quiet tones, "You have 24 hours. If I don't hear from you, I will make sure they throw the book at you so hard it breaks teeth."

I listened as he walked away. When I was sure he was out of sight I got up. The thing he'd slipped into my collar was his business card. At that point I had no intention of calling Special Agent Theodore Turdington—if that was his real name. And I also had no intention of going back to my motel room. Obviously Turdington had discovered the area where I was staying. Any number of other unsavory people could know about it by now as well. But what to do? I had a garment bag and tote bag back there. I couldn't just leave them. My best sit-down suit was in there. I figured I had to get someone totally unrelated to what was going on to go back and get my stuff. Nobody would be on the lookout for them. They could just slip in and slip out and that would be that. I'd call the motel later, tell them I'd checked out, and they could bill my card.

There was a 7-Eleven in the neighborhood, so I went and hung out in the front. Soon some teenagers came by. "Hey, excuse me," I said to them. "Do you need somebody to buy you beer?"

One of them looked at me like I was crazy. "Uh, no," he said.

Undeterred, I waited for the next profile target. A young man around 18, probably a college freshman, walked up and I proposed my offer to him.

"Yeah, sure," he said.

I explained the deal. Not only would I buy him the beer of his choice, I would pay him $20 on top of it. All he had to do was go to my motel and get my things. "My wife kicked me out of the house," I told him. "I don't want her to know where I am, but I think she found out."

"Why don't you want her to see you?" he asked.

"When you get married you'll understand." I gave him the key and directions to the motel and he was off. The kid was driving and the motel was only a few blocks away, so I figured the whole process should take no more than 10 minutes. I bided my time in the 7-Eleven parking lot, but after 15 minutes went by I started to wonder. After 20 minutes I started to worry. When 30 minutes went by and I didn't see him, I concluded I had to go back myself.

I walked a roundabout route and came around the back of the motel. Checking carefully, I moved toward my room and saw the door ajar. It was open about six inches with all the lights off inside. I didn't see the kid and I didn't know what was going on, but I wanted to get my stuff. So I took a chance and went up to the door. Standing to the side while I pushed it open, I peeked in then quickly turned on the light. I looked the place over and checked the bathroom. Everything seemed undisturbed, except that my garment and tote bags were both gone.

I didn't know what the kid was up to, but I hurried back to the 7-Eleven. When I got there, no kid. I asked inside if they'd seen anyone fitting the description and they said no. After waiting around a few minutes more, I decided I'd been ripped off, bought a 1/4 Pound Big Bite hot dog, and hopped on a bus. I was still wearing the same clothes from my run-in with the mining truck that morning, and I had to get a shower and something to put on. So I went to Kohl's, bought some business-casual attire, and then found a new motel.

18

Having also purchased yet another TracFone during my travels, I called Tyler to see if he had anything to report.

"Ahh! Dude! Where have you been? You have got to get over here, I mean right now."

"Tyler, you have to turn down the music! I can't hear you."

"Dude, it's Every Time I Die! You don't turn down Every Time I Die."

I shook my head and pressed on. "Tyler, have you heard anything new?"

"Dude, that's what I'm trying to tell you! I have to show you this. You have to come over here."

"What is it you have to show me?"

"Ahh! It's the smoking gun, dude. It's the smoking gun and Rosetta Stone rolled into one. You've got to get over here."

"You still haven't told me what it is, Tyler."

As I spoke with Tyler I also had the local news on TV and saw the Hunting Hill Quarry come up on the screen. "Tyler, hang on a second. I have to watch this."

"What? Hang up?"

The news report was about a mishap with a mining truck that had occurred earlier that day in which a person was injured and sent to the hospital. They said a Cadillac SUV had collided with the truck, which then fell over a precipice. But the report claimed it was the driver of the Cadillac who went to the hospital and that a quarry employee was driving the truck and he was uninjured. Then they did an interview with Jim and asked him about safety at the quarry.

"Sayfuss kwahree inna northeess ur millenic. Nooun dahdere fer as lung as ahkyin amaymber."

"Thank you, sir," said the reporter.

"S awite."

He apparently didn't tell anyone about me. I wasn't sure why. And they didn't identify the "driver" of the SUV, but they did say he had been taken to Shady Grove Adventist Hospital where he was in stable condition. I went back to the phone, but Tyler wasn't there. No matter, I had bigger fish to fry right now. I had to go to that hospital, get into that person's room, and find out who he was and what he knew.

I made it up to the hospital by train and bus later that evening. All this public transportation I'd been taking lately was not a problem. When I'd first started out in life insurance I drove an old beater of a car that was a) unreliable and b) not the kind of vehicle I'd want clients to see anyway. Not to mention, the cost of gas, parking—and parking tickets—made public transit competitively priced. So knowing the region's train and bus routes was second nature and this gave me a nostalgic feeling for the old days.

I walked into Shady Grove Adventist Hospital's main lobby and found the information desk. "Excuse me, young lady," I said to the elderly lady at the desk. "I'm Hank Stafford with the National American Life Insurance Company of Maryland. One of my good clients had a terrible accident in a rock quarry earlier today and he was brought here. He very much needs to see me. Can you tell me what room he's in, please?"

"Of course," she said. "What's the gentleman's name?"

"I'm sorry that's confidential. You see, he's retained me as his financial services representative and I have a fiduciary responsibility to keep his personal information private. As someone constrained by the dictates of HIPAA, I'm sure you can understand. But he's the only person injured in a rock quarry today. It made the local news."

"I'm familiar with HIPAA, sir. So you can tell me the man's name. I'm also required to keep it confidential."

"I'm sorry," I said, and then didn't move.

She paused long enough to see I was done talking, but not going anywhere. "Alright," she said, "I think I remember him." She looked at her computer monitor and scrolled through a database. "Yes, he's in room 434."

"Thanks, and what was his name?"

"Well, don't you know already?"

"Of course. I just want to make sure you've got the right person."

At this point the lady's attitude changed. "What did you say your name was again?"

"You can call me Hank."

"Do you have a business card, Hank?"

"I'm all out. I go through so many, it's hard to keep them in stock. Tell you what, I'll just go up and see my client. I'm sure everything is right."

"Just a minute, sir."

"Yes?"

"It's getting late and it really should just be close family members visiting patients around this time. You can come back tomorrow morning during the day. That should be better."

I concluded that carrying on an argument with this lady probably wouldn't work and would only end up drawing more attention than I wanted. "You're right. That's probably a better time to see him. I just hope he doesn't lose his disability coverage between now and then."

I watched the lady to see if this ploy was working. It wasn't. So I thanked her and went back outside to regroup and figure out another way in. I walked around the hospital and it seemed there were people at all the potential entrances. Then I saw a door propped open that didn't have anybody near it. I went over and looked in. It was the hospital's boiler room. I felt the outside air getting sucked in as I stood there. They must have propped the door open to help keep the place cool, but there was nothing stopping anyone from just walking in. So I did.

I walked carefully through the big, noisy room. The boilers were huge, with giant insulated ducts coming out of them. Yellow stripes were painted on the floor around the contraptions, apparently indicating a perimeter of danger. Then I was startled to see a man sitting in the corner, but felt relief when I saw he was enclosed inside a smaller, mostly glass room built into the corner of the larger room. It seemed to be air conditioned. He had his back to me with his feet up on a desk, a newspaper in his hands, and a television turned on. With the noise out in the main room, I was sure he wouldn't hear me, or see me unless he happened to turn around. The door out to the rest of the hospital was right next to his room. I simply went up to it, opened it, and went through, passing within 10 feet and in plain view of the man in the glass room.

I was now in the main part of the hospital, but where to go

from here? I knew these places were notoriously byzantine. The designers of hospitals had to be the same people who designed maze puzzles. I figured my best bet would be to get to a main-looking floor where I could appear more like a visitor looking for a room than an intruder with nefarious designs. But before I did that, I stopped into an examining room to load up on supplies, not knowing what I'd need once I confronted my tormentor. Then I found an elevator and went up one floor.

I wanted to get near main public areas without getting too close to where I'd been turned away by the nice lady at the information desk. I came to a "T" in the hallway with a sign at the end that said "Nuclear Medicine" with an arrow pointing to the right and "Lobby" with an arrow pointing to the left. Heading to the left, I stopped the first hospital employee I saw, a woman in scrubs.

"Excuse me. I'm looking for a patient's room, number 434."

"Oh, 434? Wow, how did you get way over here?"

"I don't know what happened. It's like a maze in here. I've been walking around for I don't know how long."

She then proceeded to give me directions that included eight turns, two elevators I could take along with three elevator banks I should avoid, single doors, double doors, automatic doors, doors with windows, doors without windows. I acted like I understood, said thank you and was on my way. I got as far as I could before feeling completely off the path, and I asked someone else. One more set of directions and I was there.

I saw the number "434" next to a door, and I approached. Carefully pushing it open a few inches and looking in, I saw the main lights were off with a small, dim lamp turned on. Then I saw a bed with someone in it who appeared to be asleep. I quietly went in the rest of the way. Walking slowly toward the bed I could see the person lying there was pentagram.

He was asleep and resting comfortably. I didn't see any major injuries on him—no huge bandages or casts. Whatever was wrong with him, he probably wouldn't be in that hospital long. If I was going to get any information out of him it would have to be now. So I moved the nurse's call button away from the bed and unwrapped a syringe I'd gotten from the examining room. Pulling up the plunger, I took a deep breath and thought about how this guy had dangled me from the top of the Washington Monument and tried to run me over with a 500-ton truck. I jabbed the needle into his shoulder. He winced a bit and I leaned down and said, "Hello there."

Pentagram's eyes opened and I said, "Don't move. I've got a needle stuck in your arm that's filled with air. If air gets into your blood stream it goes to your heart and stops it instantly. There's nothing anyone can do."

His eyes widened. "Get that thing out of me," he said with fear on his face.

"Are you afraid of needles?" Apparently, I'd hit on one of his phobias. I saw his hand search for the call button. "It's not there," I said. "And if you don't hold still I'm going to inject this."

"What's really in that?"

"It's air. But air will kill you faster than any poison."

"I don't believe you. That's bullshit."

"The heart's a pump. It only pumps liquid. If air gets in there the heart doesn't know what to do. It freaks out and stops. And then you're dead." I wasn't sure I was even doing the whole air-in-the-bloodstream thing right, but it seemed to be having the desired effect.

Pentagram looked at his shoulder. "Get it out," he said.

"Only after you tell me what I want to know. Answer a few

questions and I'll take it out. Where's Julia?" He was still looking anxiously at his shoulder. "Tell me or I inject this." I angled the syringe, causing him to yelp. "Quiet down. Stay quiet or this gets pushed. Who's your boss?"

"I can't tell you. Ahh, take it out."

"You've got to be kidding me. You have to be a juice head and you're afraid of needles?"

"I take supplements orally. Now take it out."

"Where's Julia?"

"I can't tell you."

Then I heard voices in the hallway. It was going to take longer with pentagram, but I didn't want to get caught pulling a Jack Bauer with this guy. "Get up," I said. "Get up now or I push this."

Pentagram got out of bed and limped with me toward the door, pulling his IV stand along with him while I held on to the syringe. I peeked out the door and saw checkers standing there arguing with a nurse.

I let go of the syringe, leaving it dangling in pentagram's shoulder, and ran out the door, heading in the opposite direction from his buddy. "Hey, wait a minute," I heard the nurse yell, and then heard checkers' footsteps coming after me. I hoped that I was more familiar with this hospital than him by now and I ran down two flights of stairs and bolted through the hallways to another staircase where I went down one more. I traced my route back toward the boiler room and began walking more calmly. I was pretty sure I'd lost checkers back at in the maze.

Opening the door to the boiler room, I walked past the man in the corner—who was now watching the American Idol season finale on TV—and back out to the world.

19

I rode a couple of buses and a train and remembered that Tyler had said he had something important to show me. So instead of going back to my motel I went over to his place.

To be safe, I went to the Target in Wheaton first and got myself a hooded sweatshirt. It was dark out and with the hood up anyone surveilling Tyler's place would think I was just one of his friends. Going down the stairs to the basement of his building, I could hear loud music as if it were right in there with me. I knocked on Tyler's door like I was the cops, so he could hear me. He opened up and a blast of noise hit me like a baseball bat to the face.

"Hank, dude! Come in!"

"I can't come in till you turn that down!"

"Dude, it's Isis. You don't turn...."

"I know, 'you don't turn down Isis.'"

"You know them?"

"No, Tyler. Just please turn that down."

Tyler complied and I went in. The place was a dump and still smelled terrible. He asked if I wanted a Dr. Pepper and I politely declined. "What is it you wanted to show me?"

"Dude, you are gonna crap yourself when you see this." He opened his computer and put in a home-burned DVD. When a picture came up it showed several people sitting in a small room. It looked like it was shot with a cell-phone camera. The picture was dark and grainy, but I could see that one of the men was wearing a military uniform. Then I took a good close look at one of the other men and it hit me. He was my Secret Service "host," the one who'd drugged me at George Will's house.

"Where did you get this?"

"A friend of mine in conspiracy research scored this."

"He gave you this DVD?"

"No, dude. He put the file up at MediaFire.com. I downloaded it and burned it myself."

I was shocked. "You got this off the internet?!"

"Relax, dude. It's not YouTube. It's very secure."

I kept watching and tried to determine what kind of uniform the first man was wearing. I could see he was a sergeant and the uniform appeared to be U.S. Army. I focused closely on the patch on his arm. It looked very much like what I'd seen when I had my sit down with Private Peter Huguenot at the Tomb of the Unknowns. It looked just like the 3rd Infantry Regiment patch, complete with the little Continental Army hat on top. This guy was with the same regiment as Todd Manderville, and he was having a conversation with the infamous "host." But there was also a third person with them. This man wore a regular business suit, and I didn't recognize him.

The sound was echoey and not real clear, so I had Tyler back it to the beginning and I tried listening more closely. "Host" and the soldier seemed to be deferring to the other man. He was the oldest of the three—in his 50s or 60s—and appeared to be running the meeting. The man said to the sergeant, "So it's very important to get our man back to base no later than the Saturday evening before Memorial Day. He'll need to be reinforced and kept in a controlled environment until go."

"Yes, sir," the sergeant replied.

"Tell me again what your procedure will be that day."

"I stay with or near our man beginning at reveille and continuing through the ceremony; the drill has been designed to accommodate our proximity needs. I check his rifle and ammo in quarters. Two hours prior to subject's arrival I administer the indication, run two safe tests, and then continue to monitor."

"Holy shit," I said.

"Alright," the man in the suit continued. "On go day you may be contacted by Major Brian Warner from DOD. This is not a mission critical contact. He's our man in the secretariat and will contact you directly only if there are last minute changes in the subject's military security. If you do not hear from this man you should continue with your current orders. Now, there has been pressure from certain investigative agencies who are not close, but need to be monitored nonetheless. You have Secret Service."

"Yes," said "host." "There's nothing on their radar at this point."

"Good."

"But...."

"But what?"

"There's a civilian who thinks he's an amateur Jim Garrison...."

"Who is he?"

"Some insurance agent. A real ninny. But he doesn't know anything. We've got him under control."

"Terminate him."

"Excuse me?" I said.

"Excuse me?" said "host."

"Terminate him. We can't take the chance."

"He doesn't know what he's doing. We have one of his girlfriends in custody and we're running disruption tactics. I believe we should stick with tradition and use the least extreme methods necessary."

"This one's too important. Tradition is changing. Terminate him."

"This must have been shot before I went to the quarry," I said.

"Dude, the shadow government's got a bull's-eye on your back," said Tyler. "You rock!"

"I wonder if that guy is Artemus Schreckengost," I said.

The group uttered a few more unremarkable things and then the video ended. By now I didn't feel like making the bus, bus, train, bus, walk back to the motel, so I asked Tyler if I could stay there.

"That's cool," he said. "But all I've got for you to sleep on is a lawn chair."

I was so tired I didn't care where I slept, so that was fine. I just asked him to please play his music at a volume in the single digits while I was there. Tyler agreed and heated up a vegan frozen pizza while the delicate noodlings of Unearth and Senses Fail bludgeoned their way out of his speakers. I went to sleep thinking of the name I'd heard the conspirators say in the video: Major Brian Warner of the DoD. I had an appointment to see Mr. Tousand at the museum the next day at noon. I thought maybe I could spend the morning tracking down this Major Warner.

The practice of running through in my mind the night before everything I wanted to accomplish the following day had become habit since I got into insurance sales. I simply transposed that practice onto solving assassination plots instead. If I could have productive sit downs with Major Warner and Mr. Tousand, I would consider it to have been a successful day. The only drawback was that I wouldn't be paid a commission for each piece of the murder plan I exposed. But I fell asleep thinking of what could amount to the mother of all commissions if I got the last piece of the puzzle in place before the plot reached its ultimate goal.

I got off the Metro at the Pentagon station around 9:00am. Arriving at the security area I was asked my business there that day. "I have an appointment to see Major Brian Warner in the secretariat."

"The Office of the Executive Secretary?" the officer asked.

"Yes, that's right."

"Your name?"

"Artemus Schreckengost." It had worked before; maybe it would work again.

"May I see a picture ID, please."

"Sure," I said, and pulled out a hot-off-the-presses phony driver's license Tyler had just whipped up for me.

The officer looked at it, wrote the name in a book, and then picked up a phone. I thought I was in, until two Pentagon police officers appeared beside me, one on each side. "Come with us, please," one of them said.

"Can I have my ID?"

"No, sir." And they took me to a room off the concourse where I sat with the two officers for some time before a more senior officer appeared.

"First of all, you're not getting into the Pentagon," the senior officer said.

"Can I ask why?"

"Sure. We have a policy against letting in anyone who shows us a fake ID."

"Ah ha!" I said. "And do you know why it's fake?"

The officers said nothing.

"I'll tell you. It's because if I used my real name I probably wouldn't be able to get in to see Major Warner."

"But..." the senior officer said, hesitating a bit, "now you tried to use a fake name and you're still not getting in to see him."

"Did you ever play poker?" I said. "Did you know that the odds of getting dealt a flush are better than the odds of getting dealt a full house? I was going for the flush."

"Thank you for that information. But now I'd like you to answer a couple questions that have nothing to do with poker, and your answers to those questions will determine whether we simply send you home or whether we arrest you and press charges."

"Charges for what? Okay, never mind."

"Let's start with your real name."

"I'm Hank Stafford."

"Do you have any ID to that effect."

"Yes." I handed over my real driver's license. I didn't give them my business card because I was beginning to think the less that this kind of thing got back to Rich Fox the better. Besides, I just wasn't in a prospecting mood—a feeling I would normally work to turn around in a jiffy. But these were Pentagon police officers on the verge of arresting me, so I kept my natural urges in check and focused on what I was there to do.

"Okay, Mr. Stafford. Why do you want to see Major Warner?"

"Sir, the purpose of my visit to Major Warner can best be explained by Major Warner himself. If I could ask you to please conduct an experiment: One of you should call Major Warner—it can be from somewhere else without me nearby—and tell him someone claiming to be Artemus Schreckengost is here to see him. You can even tell him I'm not really that person. If you do that, then you should have your answer."

"We're not interested in getting answers from Major Warner, Mr. Stafford. We're interested in getting answers from you."

At that point the room's phone rang, and one of the other officers answered it. A brief moment of surprise came over his face, and he handed the phone to the senior officer.

"Lieutenant Mullen," the senior officer said. ".... Yes, sir.... Yes, sir.... Yes, sir." And he held the phone out to me.

Not knowing quite what was going on, I hesitated a bit, but then took the phone and said, "Hello?"

"Hello, Mr. Stafford," I heard someone say in a slow-paced Southern accent. "This is Major Brian Warner. How are you doing today?"

"I'm fine, thank you," I said with apprehension. "How are you?"

"Well, I'll tell you," Warner continued in his soothing drawl. "I heard about you. I heard you're a guy who likes to have fun. And that's good. You know why that's good? Because I like to have fun too. You wanna know what I think? I think you and I are gonna have lots of fun together. Just you and me. Now what do you think of that?"

I wasn't so sure I really wanted to see this guy after all, but I said, "What kind of fun?"

"Please give the phone back to the police officer now."

I handed it back to Mullen who said into the phone, "Yes, sir.... Yes, sir.... Yes, sir," and hung up. He rose and said to the other two, "Take him into custody."

They told me to face the wall, put handcuffs on me—behind my back—and frisked me down. Then they grabbed me by the arms, a bit roughly, and led me briskly through the concourse into the Pentagon proper. They pushed me into a golf cart and we zipped through the corridors. I saw each ring designation as we whisked by: "E," "D," "C," "B," "A." We were going in toward the center. Then we went down some ramps. We went past "1" down to "M" and then to "B." Finally we stopped. We were parked outside what looked like a bank vault door. I sat in the back seat between Mullen and one of the other officers, waiting for something. Even if I could get out, there was no place to run. Then I heard a loud clank and the vault door swung open slowly and silently.

A man stepped out of the vault. "Welcome, Mr. Stafford," he said with a little smile. "I'm Major Warner." He told Mullen he would take me from there. They got me out of the cart, removed the handcuffs, and led me inside the vault door with Warner. The police officers took off in their cart and I was left alone in the basement of the Pentagon with a person I wasn't sure I'd like to be alone with in a basement anywhere. "Hank, I've got to show you something," he said as the vault door thudded closed behind us.

We walked into a suite of dimly lit concrete rooms, but there were no other people. It was totally silent in there. Major Warner pointed over his head. "Up there is the center courtyard. Between the center courtyard and you is eight feet of reinforced concrete."

"That must be heavy," I said, trying to make small talk.

"Heavy, man," Warner said. "Those walls where we came in? Six feet thick. You could slaughter a dozen hogs in here by hanging them by their little tails and giving 'em a hundred cuts with a bowie knife, and no one would ever hear a thing. Do you know how loud a hog can get when it's being slaughtered real slow?"

This was small talk I wasn't interested in pursuing. "Boy, I sure don't. I wonder if I can ask a question."

"You sure can."

"What is it you do here at the Pentagon? What's your job?"

"My job. No, I don't think I'm gonna tell you that. The point is, Hank, it just makes me think of some of the unpretty things that could happen to that pretty friend of yours if you don't pull through and do what's right."

"You mean Julia? Do you know where she is?"

"Not that I enjoy making threats, because I don't. I just want you to have all the facts clear in your head before you go and make a decision that could end up being improper."

Inside some of the rooms we walked by I could see wooden tables with straps hanging off the sides, medical equipment, and drains in the floor. I was beginning to wonder if I was going to get out of there alive. So I decided to go for broke. "Major Warner, you're not involved in a plan to kill President Obama, are you?"

"Nope," he said, putting his hand on the handle of a large metal door. "But you are." He opened the door to a room that was so dark I could barely see the other side. It was about 20 feet square, with rows of seats facing one direction. "Sit down, Hank," he said.

I sat down in one of the chairs and Major Warner left the room. There I was, alone, sealed in an almost pitch-black room under eight feet of concrete, beneath the center courtyard of the Pentagon, feeling that one of only two things was about to happen to me: hell or death. Hell because that's what being cut off from the rest of humanity is to a salesman, and death, well, that needed no further explanation. Then, suddenly, a bright light. The wall in front of me lit up, followed by a title that read "Randy Rabbit in." It was a movie. I was being shown a movie. The next title said "The Wrong Place at the Wrong Time." It turned out to be a cartoon. Major Warner apparently had locked me in this dungeon in order to show me a cartoon. I watched the story unfold.

The main character, Randy Rabbit, is walking down the street with his wife and two kids when several police cars with lights and sirens blaring drive up, and a bunch of cops jump out with guns. They force Randy to the ground, cuff him and push him into a cop car, all while his children are crying and his wife is screaming. Randy is then put in a lockup with a variety of nasty characters: a turtle that tries to rape him, an owl that tries to slash him with a razor blade, another rabbit that's mentally unbalanced and only screams and yells gibberish. Randy then is taken in front of a judge, played by a squirrel, who reads the charges against him. Randy is being charged with murdering the king elephant. Randy is shocked and tries to explain to the judge that he didn't do it. The judge says there's a lot of evidence that shows he did and that Randy will have to go on trial. He's thrown back in jail with the nasty characters who continue harassing him nonstop. Finally, the trial happens and Randy thinks he'll be able to show he had nothing to do with killing the king elephant. But during the trial, several witnesses testify they saw Randy in the area, Randy's paw prints were found on the murder weapon, and his DNA was found on the king elephant. Randy tries to refute the evidence, saying he was miles away at home with his wife at the time of the murder, and that he didn't know how his paw prints and DNA got on those things because he never touched them. The prosecution next put Randy's wife on the stand. She looked different and seemed dazed, and she testified that she couldn't remember if Randy was with her the whole time and that Randy had made negative remarks about the king elephant. The jury went out to deliberate and immediately came back, saying they had reached a verdict, which was guilty. Randy was convicted of killing the king elephant, and the judge sentenced him to death. He was handcuffed and dragged away while his children cried in the gallery. The next scene shows Randy strapped on a table with three tubes in his arm. Several characters look at him through a large window. He is asked if he has any last words and he says "I didn't do it," at which point the executioner pushes a lever and Randy goes completely still.

The wall went dark and the room went black once more. I sat alone for a minute as my eyes gradually adjusted to the dim light in the room, and I pondered what I'd just seen. Then Major Warner returned and sat next to me. "So, Hank, what did you think?"

"That was pretty disturbing."

"Aw, don't be put off by that. It's an industrial; a training film. And in this case, sometimes it's better to get the point across with allegory. Tell me you understand, Hank."

"I'm not sure I do."

"Well," Warner said, leaning in close to my face, "just let it sink in a little." He leaned back and stood. "Oh, Hank, I need to see your cell phone if you would for a minute please." He held out his hand.

I thought for a moment, but concluded refusing would probably lead to an undesirable outcome. So I handed it over. Warner pushed a few buttons and looked at the screen, and then handed the phone back. "And now," he said, "you're free to go. I wouldn't want you to be late for any of your insurance appointments."

He walked me back up to the concourse. On the way, I tried getting more information out of him, including if he knew anything about Julia. But he didn't say much. Most of the time he just kept singing the old Carol Burnett Show song "I'm so glad we had this time together...." We went past the security area where I'd been detained and Warner stopped. "I've got to get back now, Hank. You will do me a favor and do the right thing?"

"I'm sure gonna try," I said, and I headed out to the Metro station.

20

On the way back to DC my phone rang. It was Tyler and he was frantic. I didn't even hear any music in the background, so I knew something was wrong.

"Dude, where have you been! I've been trying to call!"

"Tyler, what is it? What's going on?"

"This guy trashed my place. I've been ransacked totally!"

"Who did?"

"He smashed most of my CDs and took my computer and all my burned CDs and DVDs! All my downloaded music! Even the legal stuff!"

"Tyler, slow down. Take a deep breath. You have to tell me who did it."

"I don't know. Some dude. He told me to not move or he'd break my neck. I'da pulled a ninja move on him, but he looked like the Big Show. I couldn't mess with that."

"Did he have a checker pattern shaved on the sides of his head?"

"Yes! That's the dude! How do you know him?"

"He's one of them. Now listen, you probably shouldn't stay

there anymore. I've got to go talk to somebody. But this phone isn't safe, so don't call this number again. I'm going to have to call you back."

Somehow they knew about Tyler. I guessed it was only a matter of time. But now he was a target as well, and I felt guilty. I had to get to the bottom of this before more innocent people got caught up. I bought yet another TracFone, then called Tyler back and told him to meet me on the Mall in front of the Air and Space Museum in an hour.

Out of all the people I'd spoken with so far, only this Mr. Tousand had knowledge of the plot and was willing to talk to me. Praying he could help, I walked into the museum just after noon and asked for him at the desk. The woman asked my name, so I told her I was "Dirk Muncie of the Howard Hughes Spruce Goose Society." She made a call, and told me to wait in the Milestones of Flight exhibit. I walked across to where the museum kept early spacecraft and airplanes, and waited under Charles Lindbergh's Spirit of St. Louis. Shortly, Mr. Tousand appeared, walking briskly to my location. He seemed agitated.

"Mr. Stafford, hello. Thank you for coming. I don't have much time. I just wanted to tell you I appreciate your interest in what's going on. I would like to help you; I truly would. But I've thought it over and I just can't. This isn't something I can do right now."

This wasn't what I wanted to hear, so I went into answering-objections mode. "Mr. Tousand, let me ask you a question. Do you feel there are people who would be better off if this plot were not allowed to go forward?"

"Yes, certainly."

"And do you feel you have something to contribute that could help stop this plot?"

"Mr. Stafford, perhaps. But I don't think you are the one I should be confiding in."

"If not me, then who? Who will you be talking to within the next two days that can help stop needless pain and suffering?"

Tousand began to get heated. "Mr. Stafford, I know what you're trying to do and it won't work. I've already told you I can't help you."

"Sir, have I offended you? If I've done anything to upset you, I apologize."

"No, you haven't," Tousand said, still agitated. "Please don't take it personally, I just don't think it will do any good."

I saw that our animated discussion was drawing attention. One man in particular was staring at us the entire time. He looked Middle Eastern or maybe Asian; he had a beard, and wore a frock coat and furry hat. But I had to win Tousand over. "Mr. Tousand, please believe me. I don't take it personally, and I understand how you feel. I'm sure many people in your position would feel the same way, though there probably aren't a lot of people in your position. But if there were, I'm sure they would find if they told me what they knew, brought me into their confidence, accepted me as a partner and teammate in this fight for the right thing, that they would be able to sleep better at night knowing they tried to make the country more secure and better protected."

"That's fine, Mr. Stafford. But who are you? You're an insurance salesman. You can't even protect yourself. You've almost been killed already. And sooner or later they will succeed, but not before they've gotten out of you everyone you've talked to and what they told you. No, I'm sorry, you can't be trusted."

Here I got a little angry. "Excuse me, sir. I didn't get where I am in my business by being untrustworthy. I don't just sell insurance. I manage my clients' financial needs from cradle to grave, which they wouldn't allow me to do if I was untrustworthy."

Now, in addition to the Middle Eastern man staring at us, another person began walking directly toward us. A woman. She was in my line of sight, appearing over Tousand's left shoulder and coming up directly behind him. But I tried to stay focused on Tousand. He said, "Alright, alright," and paused. "I'll tell you what you want to know. I know everything. I know who's involved and what their general planning is. I know your friend at the Secret Service; I know about your visit to see Major Warner. I know them all."

"What about Turdington?" I asked as I glanced over Tousand's shoulder to look at the approaching woman. Even though she wore sunglasses and a hooded coat with long, baggy sleeves, I could see that she was Susan Underhill.

"Not here...." Tousand uttered as Susan, without breaking stride, passed next to him and raised her arm. I heard a loud pop. She took two more steps, turned, and screamed as a gun hit the floor between Tousand's feet and mine, and Tousand himself fell like a tree over to one side, hitting the floor with a sickening thud.

Tourists turned and gasped. The Middle Eastern man began shouting his head off in some foreign language as he pointed in my direction. I looked down at Tousand who had red liquid oozing out of his head, and looked very dead. There was general uproar. Susan Underhill had stepped back with the rest of the crowd; I didn't think anyone had seen her do it. The Middle Eastern man kept shouting and pointing at me.

I asked a younger man in western dress standing next to him, "What is he saying?"

"We are from Turkmenistan. He no speak English."

"Why is he pointing at me?"

"He think you shoot that man."

"Did you see me shoot him?"

"No, I see nothing."

I looked straight ahead and saw security guards running my way. I had a feeling if it was going to be my word against the Turkmen's, I would lose. He must have thought Tousand and I were arguing and then I shot him. So I turned and ran. I ran out of the museum and across the Mall as fast as I could. By the time I got to the other side I could hear police sirens.

Not knowing where I was going, a crazy thought went through my head. If I could get to FBI headquarters and find Tyler's father, I figured, maybe somehow he could help. The FBI building was close, just over at 9th Street and Pennsylvania Ave. When I got there I slowed down. Trying to look casual, I walked around the building while I tried to think of an approach before going in. Suddenly, I heard the same shouting Turkmen from back at the museum. I looked to the street and there he was, hanging out the window of a police cruiser ardently pointing in my direction, while a cop got out of the driver's side.

Abandoning my FBI idea, I darted across E Street and slipped into a building with no windows on the first floor. There were people inside, so I ducked into a small corridor. Thinking the police would surely look into all the buildings along this street, I needed to get to a better hiding place and found a curved staircase going to the second floor. Sneaking down another narrow hallway, I quietly opened a door and slipped inside what looked like a good-sized closet. It seemed like I could hide there until things simmered down.

It wasn't long, though, and I heard footsteps and voices coming up the stairs and down the hall. There was a door on the other side of the closet, and I carefully opened it to see what was inside. But what I saw was totally unexpected. I was looking through a small balcony into a theater. Then it hit me. This was Ford's Theatre. And I was in the presidential box. Lincoln's box. But before I had a chance to admire history, someone came through the doorway from the hall.

"Hey, you!" he shouted.

I ran into Lincoln's box and peered over the railing to the stage. Looking behind me I saw two cops and a theater employee coming in. There was nowhere to go but down. So I climbed over the railing and jumped for the stage, but my foot got caught in the bunting draped in front of the box, and I hit the stage awkwardly. I got up and shouted to my pursuers, "I didn't shoot him! It was Susan Underhill!"

I'd twisted my ankle in the fall and ran with a limp backstage. Seeing a way out the back of the theater, I grabbed a costume off a rack and went out. I ended up in a series of alleyways in the center of the block, where I quickly put on the costume hat and switched jackets. The costume jacket was large enough for me to stuff my own underneath, making me look like a much heavier man. I followed an alley out and found myself on 9th Street. There was a Metro station over at 7th Street and Pennsylvania Ave. If I could get on a train, I figured I'd have half a chance of getting where I'd be more safe. But during my nonchalant stroll to that intersection, my phone rang. It was Tyler.

"Dude, where are you? That museum is crawling with cops!"

"I'm on 7th Street near Penn Ave. Where are you?"

"I'm near Penn Ave on 7th Street."

I looked to my left and there was Tyler sitting in a ten-year old Toyota Corolla waiting at the traffic light on 7th Street and Indiana Ave. I approached his car.

"Dude, don't even ask me for directions. I'm lost too."

"Tyler, it's me. Hank."

"Hank, dude! What are you dressed up for?"

"Never mind. Just drive me out of here fast."

The passenger seat was covered with clothing, papers, CDs, and garbage of all sorts. Tyler grabbed most of it and threw it in the back, though he kept one CD. I got in as he was putting it in his player. The light was green by now and cars behind us began to honk.

"Tyler, let's move it."

"Give me a sec. I'm putting on Homewrecker by Converge. I love driving fast to this song."

Loud, fast, dissonant, shrieking metallic punk rock blared out of the car's distorting speakers as Tyler peeled away from the traffic light.

"Tyler," I shouted. "I don't want to draw attention to us!" But it was no use, he was in a zone. His muffler sounded like a miniature Harley and he laid a patch at every traffic light. If the cops weren't all busy looking for a murderer, we'd be in trouble.

He headed up New York Ave and out of the city. On the way I told him what had happened.

"That's where you went at the airport? You hooked up with some chick who kills people? Dude, that's intense!"

I didn't wonder where Tyler was going until he got to the Beltway and headed south. I asked and he said, "The last place the cops and conspirators would think to look."

"Where's that?"

"Six Flags America!"

21

The big amusement park in the DC area, Six Flags was just over in Mitchellville. It was not where I would have picked to lay low, but Tyler was probably right about no one thinking to look there. And hanging out there for a while would give me time to think, even though time was running out and my prospects were crapping out left and right—one literally dying right in front of me.

If I'd had this kind of luck selling life insurance, I wouldn't have been in the game for long. Getting the interview was the hard part. Once I got face to face with a prospect it was practically a done deal. I had one of the highest closing ratios in my office. But this was different. This was real omerta-type stuff. If people followed my lead here, they weren't signing up to have $300 per month automatically deducted from their checking accounts; they were risking having a bullet crash through their skulls.

There were only a few people at the park when we got there —it was a Thursday early in the season—making it harder to get lost in the crowd. But as soon as we ventured in Tyler took over like he lived there, rattling off a list of all the rides he wanted to go on, and knowing where everything was without looking at a map.

First stop, Superman: Ride of Steel, the big roller coaster with a 200-foot first hill and an almost vertical drop. Tyler was ecstatic.

"The first time I rode this, I went on 14 times straight!"

"That's quite an accomplishment," I said.

As we waited in line for the next ride, I heard someone yell Tyler's name. "Yo, Tyler!" "Hey, poser!" We looked and saw three young men with shaved heads standing just outside the line-up area. "Hey, Tyler," one of them yelled. "Why don't you go X up at a Slayer show!"

"Who are those guys?" I asked.

"SHARPs."

"Sharps? What's that?"

"Skin Heads Against Racial Prejudice. They're like Nazis without any of the bad stuff."

"No, I mean how do they know you?"

"Just from around, from shows and stuff. They're good guys. They can just be assholes sometimes."

"Tyler," yelled one of the SHARPs, "I saw you online last night. Your screen name was 'X-dweeb-X.'"

"Hey, Kurt!" Tyler yelled. "I saw a picture of you online last night. You were eating a bag of dicks!"

"Tyler," came the retort. "Why don't you listen to music from this century? We're sick of you talking about bands that broke up five years ago."

"He doesn't know what he's talking about," Tyler explained to me. "My older brother got me into hardcore when I was 12. I still love the old bands." Then he shouted so his tormentors could hear, "But I bet they never even heard of Mogwai!"

"Mogwai?!" they exclaimed and all broke out laughing. "Is that what you listen to when you get sand in your vagina?"

"Yeah, that's funny. Hey, why don't you put on your skinny

suspenders and go back to listening to Max Resist."

"You wanna dance, Tyler?"

"No, I don't believe in cheap shots."

"No cheap shots. We won't do any of that."

With this, Tyler jumped over the railings of the line-up area one by one to confront his antagonizers just as the gate was being opened to let in the next group. "Tyler," I shouted after him, "forget about it!" Before I could turn to go after him, a man came up from behind and gave me a push. I felt something in my ribs and looked down. I saw a gun being jabbed into my side. I looked up and it was checkers.

"If you don't go," he said, "I'll either shoot you or turn you in to the cops. Your choice."

So I went. He directed me to the back of the coaster. It wasn't full and everyone else tried to get as close to the front as they could. Checkers and I sat in the very last car. A yellow lap bar secured us in and the coaster started on its way. I didn't know what checkers was up to. I didn't know if he'd gotten me into this secure spot to offer me a deal or to keep me immobilized while they pursued another part of their plan. And how did he even know I was there?

The coaster went slowly up the first hill. It seemed to take forever, being a 200-foot vertical rise. About two thirds of the way up, I suddenly felt a sharp blow to my right temple. I was dazed, but awake, and I could see checkers reach down and release something at the base of the lap restraint. The thing popped loose, and as we approached the top of the hill, checkers pushed me over and began lifting me out. I tried to hold on with my left leg, and when he saw I wasn't unconscious he pulled me back and gave me a couple more blows to the head. I could hear screaming as the front of the coaster started over the hill. Checkers again tried to lift me out. Hanging over the side I could see the ground 20 stories below. Then the speed of the coaster picked up dramatically. It started down the other side of the hill and I felt suddenly weightless. Being dazed and limp, and having no lap restraint, my body started rising up out of my seat. Checkers gave me one more push, but instead of guiding me over the side, the shove made me airborne above the seats. I hovered for a split second over checkers' head. Just as the coaster was reaching the bottom I threw my arms around checkers' neck as the coaster started to speed horizontally at over 70 miles per hour. Had I not made that move, the coaster's forward motion would have left me behind and crashing into the tracks. As it was, even though I'd been knocked nearly unconscious, the adrenaline rush let me get a tight grasp with both arms.

Immediately, the coaster went into a fast, sharp right turn, the centrifugal force pulling me to the side. I could hear checkers groan at the strain on his neck and head. He was so busy trying to keep his head attached and body inside the coaster he didn't even try to get my arms off. But as soon as the coaster straightened and slowed a bit, I fell back into the seat and he started punching at me again. I would not, however, release my grip. This was the only thing keeping me alive and him somewhat incapacitated.

As the coaster went down the second hill I got my legs out and moved around behind checkers. Another hard right turn—this time going completely around one and half times—and checkers' head was like a dock post straining to hold the ship against rough seas. We went through several more hills and turns with me hanging off the back of the coaster while holding on to checkers' neck. We finally pulled back into the boarding area and came to a stop. I dropped off the coaster and climbed onto the platform, strolling out as quickly but nonchalantly as I could. Glancing back, I could see checkers gasping for breath and checking his neck for damage.

On the way, I stopped at the photo counter. These rides always had a camera taking pictures of each seat at some thrilling point in the ride so that people could purchase a memento of the experience. In my case, getting a picture showing checkers and what was going on could have been vital evidence. But when I asked the cashier about the picture from my location, she said it had been deleted. She showed me the complete set from that ride and two of them had been blanked out, my seat and one other. She said they'll do that because some of the riders know where the camera is and will make obscene gestures as their picture is getting snapped. A hell of a lot went on during that trip, but an obscene gesture I didn't think had been one of them. However, I didn't have time to argue. The picture was gone and that was that. I got out of there as quickly as I could and began looking for Tyler.

As I searched through the park it struck me the only way checkers could have known my location was through Tyler. It was his idea to go to Six Flags and I knew we weren't followed. The fear and adrenaline made my mind race and I began thinking no one was trustworthy. It seemed like Amber was setting me up in some kind of insurance-fraud sting; Ted Turdington was either an FBI agent or he wasn't, but either way I was screwed; Susan Underhill turned out to be one of them; and who was Tyler? He was some kid I hardly knew, who I met through Amber, who I was now thinking couldn't be trusted. And what about Todd? The only real evidence I had on his connection to an assassination plot had been Amber's description. Something was obviously going on, but what? What did I really know for sure? Nothing. Yet I was being chased by the cops for murder, being chased by murderers who were trying to kill me, being dogged by some deranged maybe FBI agent for attempted murder and insurance fraud. And I hadn't done anything except maybe be in the wrong place at the wrong time. This last thought made me stop short in my tracks.

I looked toward the exit from The Joker's Jinx ride and there was Tyler coming out with the three SHARPs. They were laughing and acting like the best buddies in the world. I approached and told Tyler I had to talk to him. Tyler bade the others farewell, shook their hands, and they headed off toward the Batwing.

"What is this? I thought you were enemies."

"No, dude. Like I said, they're cool. We're all going to see the Cro-Mags next week."

"Anyway, I need to talk to you." I took Tyler around to a more secluded spot.

Looking me over he said, "What happened to you?"

"That roller coaster is an awesome ride," I said, and asked him the question. "Did you let anybody know where you were taking me today?"

"No, dude. Of course not."

"Then how did that guy with the checker haircut know I was here?"

"Whoa, that guy's here?"

"Yes, and there's no way he could have known unless somebody told him."

"Hank, dude. You think I told him? He harassed me too."

"But I don't know that for sure. I don't know anything for sure."

"Okay, I got an idea. Name all the suspicious people you've come in contact with since this whole thing began."

That could have been everyone I'd met, but I played along. "Well, there's Amber, there's the guy from the National Threat Assessment Center at the Secret Service, there's Todd Manderville, Ted Turdington, Susan Underhill, checkers and pentagram, Major Brian Warner, maybe you...."

"Damn, dude. You get around!"

I shrugged. "It's the nature of my business."

"So is there a chance any of those people—except me 'cause I know I didn't—is there a chance any of them planted a tracking device on you?"

"I don't know. I was unconscious one night at George Will's house."

"George Will?"

"Never mind. I don't think he's involved. I don't think so, anyway. Checkers, pentagram and my host from the Secret Service where all there and...."

"You should get an X-ray."

"Why an X-ray?"

"You ever see Jackass?"

"Is that a band?"

"No, it's a movie."

"I haven't seen it."

"You should. It's effing hilarious."

"What does that have to do with anything?"

"They could have slipped something inside of you, something that would only show up on a X-ray."

"Slipped something inside.... I wonder...." I had a thought and lifted my shirt. "Tyler, look at the middle of my upper back. Do you see anything?"

He looked and said, "Yeah, there's like a big scratch there."

"Feel underneath it. Do you feel anything in there?"

He pushed at the area, which hurt like hell. "I don't know, dude. Wait a minute. I think I feel something. Yup, something's definitely in there."

I put my shirt down and suggested we go to the men's room. When we got into a stall Tyler went back to inspecting the area.

"It hasn't scarred over yet," Tyler said. "I think I can get it out." At which point he produced a pocket knife, and was about to stick it in my back.

"Wait a minute! What are you doing? Wash that thing off with soap first."

He did so, then came back and started to dig. As I grimaced and clenched my teeth, I heard someone come into the men's room. The dialogue that emerged from the stall must have been choice, but I didn't want to wait. I wanted that thing out.

"Ow, that hurts. Are you sure you washed it good?"

"Yeah, dude, I washed it. Just hold still; it's almost in."

I groaned and grunted.

"Hold still," said Tyler, "I'm almost there."

"Go faster," I said.

Whoever was out there came up to our stall door. I could see the shadow of his legs on the floor.

"Whoa, dude. You're starting to bleed."

I grunted and groaned some more.

"I'm close, I'm close, I'm close!" said Tyler.

I heard the person outside our stall mutter "Jesus, that's sickening," and then walk away.

I pulled Tyler down and whispered, "See who that is."

He peeked over the top of the stall and shot back down. "Holy crap, it's checkers."

"What's he doing?"

"He's leaving."

"Good. Hurry up and get this thing out."

Tyler went in one more time and pulled out the object. It was about the size of a piece of long-grain rice. "There's your transmitter," Tyler said.

"Susan Underhill," I said.

"How'd she get that in there without you knowing?"

"Never mind. Let's get out of here."

We moved carefully through the park. Tyler knew the place inside and out, and we were able to go around and behind rides and buildings for the most part. Just before leaving we saw Kurt and the other SHARPs one more time.

"So Tyler, don't bring your mom to the show like you did last time," Kurt said.

"I won't, dude. Later."

When we were safely back in Tyler's car I asked him what he did with the transmitter.

"Let's just say Kurt is going to have some unexpected company for a while."

22

I didn't know where to go. I was both agitated and depressed. I needed a drink. When we got near FedExField, the home of the Redskins, I told Tyler to pull off the highway and we went to the Boulevard at the Capital Centre where we headed into the Sideline Bar & Grill.

The bartender asked for Tyler's ID and he said, "Dude, I don't even drink alcohol. I'm straight edge."

"I don't care if you're a paint edger; I still need to see ID."

"Alright, dude. Don't hassle me." Tyler gave the bartender an ID.

"This says you're 26."

"It does? Well anyway, dude, I don't drink alcohol. All I want is a Mountain Dew."

I had to interject. "Excuse me. He doesn't drink alcohol, but I do. My doctor says I need to drink lots of alcohol and if I miss my dose I could get renal failure and seizures."

The bartender finally went and got our drinks, Tyler's Mountain Dew and I had a gin and tonic.

"So what does that mean," I asked, "being 'straight edge'?"

"It means I don't drink, don't smoke, don't do drugs. I keep my mind clear and focused so I can fulfill my true potential. I don't believe in sex outside a serious monogamous relationship because I respect women and don't need the distraction. And I don't eat meat. Meat production is cruel, unsustainable, and unnecessary."

"Is that a religion?"

"Nope. It's just a way of life. There are Christian straight edgers, atheist straight edgers, and everyone else. We all get along because we believe in mutual respect."

I ordered another gin and tonic as Tyler went on about the counterproductive effects of alcohol.

"So what got you into assassination research?" I asked.

"My dad works at the FBI, and one time when I was a kid I heard these voices coming out of his office at home. So I opened the door and looked in and the voices were coming from a tape recording. My dad was in there listening to it. I asked him what it was, and he said it was a recording of a police interrogation of a witness after Robert Kennedy was shot. So the witness is a woman who was in the room when the shooting happened, and she's trying to tell the cop that there were shots fired from other directions, not just from Sirhan Sirhan. And she's trying to describe somebody she saw. But this cop from the LAPD is just menacing the crap out of her. He's insulting her, telling her she's lying, yelling and screaming. He's telling her she's disgracing the memory of Bobby Kennedy. He's doing everything he can to get her to change her story. I asked my dad why he was listening to that, and he said he was in training and researching examples of police interrogation, you know, examples where they do it right and examples where they do it wrong. So I say to him 'Is this an example of how to do it right?' He didn't answer at first, but then he said 'No, it isn't.' And he turned off the tape player and told me not to ask him about that stuff anymore."

"Is your dad involved in researching or investigating assassinations?"

"No. At least not that I know of. He seemed kind of freaked by the whole thing and just wants to do his job. He doesn't want to go digging up the past. So that's why I got into it. I became the researcher for my family!"

I revisited our current situation. "I have to wonder what these people were thinking," I said. "Don't they know that people would ask why a person who just committed a murder in the middle of Washington would go all the way to Six Flags and jump off the top of a roller coaster?"

"People will ask, dude. But they'll never get an answer. That's how it's set up."

"So what can we do now? Can we download your friend's video file again?"

"Oh, I forgot to tell you! They ransacked his place too. It's not even up at MediaFire anymore."

"Shit. Now what?" I pondered that question as I drank down two more gin and tonics. I was getting pretty tight by now. Fortunately, I didn't do this very often. I could count on the fingers of one hand the number of times I drank that much over the course of a year. I agreed with Tyler that one could not be at the top of his game while drinking, and with all the evening work in my business, it just wasn't practical. Where I disagreed with Tyler was that there were times—such as after seeing someone get their brains blown out one foot from your face, being chased by the cops for it, and dangling off the back of a speeding roller coaster 200 feet above the ground—when getting a good drunk on was not such a bad idea.

"Did I ever tell you The Theory?" I asked. "I mean really tell you The Theory?"

"Yeah, like how lone nuts weren't all responsible for those assassinations, and how John Dean was knocked off to send a message."

"That's fine. But did I go over the means, motive, and opportunity? All the details?"

Tyler thought for a second, and said, "Nope," which turned out to be mistake.

I ordered another gin and tonic for me and Mountain Dew for Tyler, and then—with the bartender making it an audience of two—launched into a drunken exposition of The Theory that was one for ages:

"Okay. The thing of it is, the United States emerged from World War II the only major power not laid waste by the war, standing for the first time as the preeminent nation on earth. A sense of urgency—as well as an inflated ego—surely followed this new-found status. The country now had both the opportunity and the right, some might think, to protect its hegemony by whatever means necessary."

The bar was not close to full, but there were a few other patrons, and I'd begun to attract their attention.

"Enter the CIA. Developed after World War II, the agency was given huge resources and the task of developing ways to maintain the advantage over adversaries... secretly. By 1961, the agency had been diligently honing its skills for eight years under director Allen Dulles, skills that included ways to assassinate heads of state. Then Dulles was fired by John F. Kennedy who apparently intended to reign in and restructure the agency. The 18-year period begins two years later, with Kennedy its first victim."

My audience had grown to five, which only served to encourage me.

"Presidents and presidential candidates represent the most

direct control of—or threat to—political power. Lyndon Johnson took over from Kennedy and proceeded to greatly escalate the conflict in Vietnam, proving to be a prodigious hawk where the Cold War was concerned. But after four years, things were not going as well as had been hoped, and the Tet Offensive in January 1968 was the tipping point that turned the public very much against the war."

By now I was standing on a chair, and the audience had grown to seven.

"The presidential election was coming that November and Johnson knew he was in trouble. On March 12, he narrowly beat out anti-war candidate Eugene McCarthy in the Democrats' first primary. Four days later, JFK's brother Robert Kennedy—also anti-war, but wildly popular—entered the race. Johnson, seeing the handwriting on the wall and wanting to avoid the embarrassment of being an incumbent president who failed to receive his own party's nomination, announced on March 31 that he was dropping out of consideration for reelection as president."

"What a pussy!" someone yelled.

"You betcha. But four days later, Martin Luther King, Jr., who had begun speaking out against the war, was assassinated. Fifteen percent of the war's U.S. combat fatalities had been African American. The man who had shepherded the Civil Rights Act of 1964—as well as the 'Great Society'—was effectively resigning, leaving the increasingly anti-war King as the nation's most respected national leader to black Americans. If he persuaded this significant portion of the draft-age population to shun the war, it could create a crisis for those determined to carry it on."

"Testify, brother," someone said, as I now had nine onlookers.

"Two months after King was shot, following his victory in

the California primary—a victory that indicated he had a serious chance at winning the nomination—Robert Kennedy was also gunned down. Later that summer, Johnson's pro-war vice president Hubert Humphrey received the Democratic nomination for president."

"Booooo!" came the reply.

"And then Republican Richard Nixon, who promised to bring the war to conclusion through victory, went on to win the election. It was close, but Humphrey wasn't Nixon's biggest concern. The most serious threat to Republican victory in 1968, as well as to victories in the foreseeable future, was embodied in a man named George Wallace, the governor of Alabama."

"Sweet home Alabama!" came the commentary.

"Beginning in 1880 and going through 1960—a total of 21 presidential elections—no state from the Deep South had ever gone for a Republican candidate. South Carolina, Georgia, Alabama, Mississippi, and Arkansas were so pissed off at Republicans for the Civil War that they consistently denied the party their electoral votes for 80 straight years. Add Louisiana, which went Republican only once in that time period, and you have a formidable block. If Democrat John F. Kennedy had not received any electoral votes from those states in 1960 he would not have gotten the required majority."

"Get this guy his own show!" Someone said, as everyone in the place was now watching.

"But all that changed with Lyndon Johnson. President Johnson's promotion and signing of the Civil Rights Act of 1964 was a stab into the heart of those who ruled the South. On top of that, Johnson's opponent in the election that year was Republican Barry Goldwater, a man who stood for individual rights and was dead-set against what he perceived to be undue acquisitions of power by the federal government. He came out against the Civil Rights Act, not—he'd said—because he was for segregation, but because he saw it as an unconstitutional imposition of federal power over the states. Either way, the South now had a new best friend, and from that moment on—for the first time since Reconstruction—Republicans had a shot at winning the electoral votes of the South."

"Let's start another Civil War!"

"Not so fast. One man stood in their way. In the 1968 presidential election, third-party candidate George Wallace won the electoral votes of Georgia, Alabama, Mississippi, Louisiana, and Arkansas, plus one vote from North Carolina where he came in second to Nixon. He also came in second to Nixon in Tennessee and South Carolina. And though coming in third behind Nixon and Humphrey in Florida and Virginia, Wallace still managed to get 29% and 24% of the vote, respectively."

Several in the audience had started up their own entertainment, belting out Lynyrd Skynyrd's "Sweet Home Alabama," with its line "In Birmingham they love the governor, boo boo boo!" So I got louder.

"In 1972, Wallace showed no signs of slowing down. His tactic this time was to try to get the Democratic nomination along with its major-party support. Initial signs looked good as he not only won the Florida primary on March 14, he won every county in the state. He came in second in Wisconsin, showing appeal outside the South, then went on to win the Tennessee and North Carolina primaries. He came in second in West Virginia and then on May 15 he was shot multiple times by Arthur Bremer while campaigning in Maryland. The following day he won the Maryland and Michigan primaries."

"Now there's a man!"

"Ahh, but Wallace was done. Recovering from his injuries took time and he had been permanently paralyzed from the waist down. That fall, Richard Nixon won every state that Wallace had taken in 1968."

More singing: "Turn out the lights, the party's over...."

"And so it went. Republicans took control of the South from that point on, and it seemed the only way Democrats could win a presidential election was to nominate somebody from the region, i.e., Jimmy Carter and Bill Clinton. That is, until Barack Obama."

"Number 44. Reggie Jackson!"

I was winding myself up for the final flourish, the presentation of the facts that proved how Obama was such a threat to the power structure... when I fell off my chair. Laughter and applause greeted the stunt. Several people helped me up, one of them saying, "That was better than Lucky's monologue."

"Thank you," I replied, though I wasn't sure what he was talking about. I'd lost count of the number of gin and tonics I drank, but what I remembered clearly was the idea that popped into my head next. "Joe Lieberman!" I blurted out.

Tyler, himself on his fourth Mountain Dew, almost jumped out of seat. "What are you trying to do to me, dude?"

"So, Tyler, listen to me. I'll tell you something for nothing. Hear me now, believe me later. The Secret Service, maybe FBI and local police are compromised and I don't feel safe going to them. But chances are real good they don't have congressmen in on this. It wouldn't make sense. Right? They don't need them. Why go through the trouble of infiltrating an organization when you don't need to?"

"Joe Lieberman?" said Tyler.

"Joe Lieberman is the chairman of the Senate Homeland

Security and Governmental Affairs Committee. These crimes are his jurisdiction. If I can get to him and explain to him everything I know and everything that's been happening to me. Then maybe he'll help out. He can bring to bear the full investagive.. investagive... anyway, resources of the United States Senate, and there's nothing those other agencies can do about it."

"But, dude...."

"Tyler, listen to me. In any of your assassination research, have you ever seen evidence of congress being involved in a plot? It's always the CIA, FBI, Secret Service, police departments, the military. Dig it. These are all executive branch agencies. Executive branch. Congress isn't part of that. It's an entirely separate branch."

"What about Gerald Ford?"

"What about him?"

"He was a congressman when he was on the Warren Commission. And it turned out he was a mole for the FBI. He told J. Edgar Hoover everything the Warren Commission was doing behind closed doors, including when other commissioners were doubting the idea of a single shooter from the School Book Depository."

"Tyler," I said, putting my arm around his shoulders. "Tyler, Gerry Ford was acting on his own. He was the lone nut on the Warren Commission. He wasn't acting in his official capacity as a member of the United States House of Representatives. The institution is unsullied. I'm gonna go see Joe Lieberman."

I left a tip on the bar, put on my costume jacket and hat, and started out.

"Hank," Tyler said, coming after me, "you can't go down there. Every cop in DC is looking for you. The capitol ain't someplace you can just walk into without being noticed."

"Tyler, the capitol building is a house like any other. There's a front door, and there's a person on the other side who decides whether to let you in. The worst thing that can happen to a door-to-door salesman is to find nobody home. If somebody answers the knock on the door, then there's opportunity. And what is opportunity? She's a mistress to be romanced, caressed, and bedded." I looked at my watch. "It's getting late. Do you want to drive me or do I have to walk to the Largo Town Center Metro stop?"

"I'll take you, dude. Either you get in to see Senator Joe Lieberman or you get arrested by a hundred cops. I don't want to miss that!"

23

On the way the Capitol, I had Tyler turn down the Stormtroopers of Death so I could check my voicemails at home and work. There were a total of eight messages from Peggy. They alternated between frantic, sobbing fears of the worst and relieved, hopeful indications she'd gotten from the police and others. Ultimately, though, there was nothing new to report. Julia was still missing and nobody knew where she was.

There was also a message from Rich Fox, saying he had something he needed to discuss with me. Then the last message began with a prolonged sigh, and went "Good afternoon, Hank. This is Special Agent Theodore Turdington. It looks to me like you chose to ignore the deadline we agreed to. You do not want to ignore me, Hank. You really, really don't. Call me when you get this message. Better yet, call me before you get this message."

He hadn't said anything about the shooting at the museum. It could have meant he didn't know about it because either he called before the information got to him or because he wasn't really an FBI agent and privy to the info. Or, and this would have been the much preferred scenario, nobody knew the identity of the person who ran from the scene. I needed to find out for sure, so I instructed Tyler to stop at the public library at the intersection of Capitol Street and Central Ave.

He came to a screeching halt in the library parking lot, taking up two spaces, and we ran for the door. A surprised library employee, who was just coming to the door to lock it, stepped back as we barged in. "Excuse me, we're closing," he said. At which point he felt the full barrage of the Tyler/drunk-Hank sales team.

"We've got to look something up on the internet. It'll take two seconds!" Tyler said.

"I'm sorry, sir, for the lateness of our arrival," I started, "but he's right. We have an urgent, immediate need to look something up online that we promise will not take more than two minutes of your time."

"The library closes at 5:30. Those are the rules," said the employee.

"Dude, you're not serious. We got in before 5:30."

"No, no, no. He's right," I said to Tyler. "He has a job he needs to do. And he doesn't know about your lottery ticket." Then turning my attention to the employee. "You see, we're late getting home to his mom and we're pretty sure they just called the Hot Lotto winning number, which my boy here has in his possession. If we could just spend one minute to get on the computer and verify that he really has the winning ticket for two million dollars, then we could give his mom the best surprise of her life. She would be so happy. Could you please help us this one time?"

"Yeah, dude. I'm gonna video her reaction and put it on YouTube!"

"And when we get interviewed by the press, I'll be sure to mention the library employee who made the most joyous feeling of a lifetime possible for one loving, wheelchair-bound woman."

"Alright," the employee said, "try to be quick. If you're still there in three minutes I'm going to ask you to leave."

"Thank you, sir," I said.

"Thanks, dude. I'm gonna give you part of the jackpot!"

I grabbed Tyler and we sat at a computer terminal. I first checked the U.S. Senate site and found the location of Lieberman's office. Then, checking the Washington Post online, I read their story about the museum shooting. There was no mention of me by name. They had the name I'd given at the desk—"Dirk Muncie"—and they had a good description. But that was it. I decided as long as I kept wearing the disguise, I'd be in good shape. But then another story caught my eye: "Police Close Case in Death of John Dean."

The medical examiner's report had come out and it concluded John Dean had died of natural causes. The examiner and the police said they had conducted an exhaustively thorough investigation and had concluded there was no foul play or anything else suspicious about this death.

"Alright, time's up," came the library employee.

"Uh, thanks," I said. "We're done."

"So, did you win?"

"No, uh, the ticket turned out to be from a different day. But thank you for your time."

"But if I ever do win," added Tyler, "I'm gonna remember you."

The findings in the Dean death only ended up doing what so many of the facts in these assassination plots did, which was to fail to prove a plot while also failing to prove that one did not exist. Obviously, events had transpired in the interim that rendered the cause of Mr. Dean's demise moot, and I soldiered on in my quest to see Senator Joe Lieberman.

We parked near the Hart Senate Office Building. I didn't notice if Tyler had parked legally, but chances were in this part of DC he hadn't. We went to the Constitution Ave entrance of the Hart building where Lieberman had his office and found it locked.

"It's late," said Tyler. "They must be closed."

"Congress is in session," I said. "And they like to work late." I saw a security guard inside and waved to him. He took a good long look at me, and then said something into his radio. He went back to watching me, and the door did not open. Then I saw a police officer walking down the sidewalk toward us. I decided I could start pounding on the door, cause a scene and get arrested, or make a tactful retreat. So we crossed Constitution Ave and headed up the narrow, curved part of Maryland Ave toward the Capitol.

"I'll go to the senate side," I said, "And explain I've got a national security issue I need to discuss with Senator Lieberman."

"Are you sure you don't need an appointment for that?"

"An appointment? Let me tell you something about making appointments with people in official positions. You call them at the phone number listed for them, but you don't get to talk to them directly. You talk to their secretary. First of all, try explaining to a secretary that elements of the government who are trying to kill the president almost threw you off a roller coaster. Second, what usually happens is the secretary takes your information and then says either she or the official will call you right back. And then you never hear from them again. Third, even if you do manage to book an appointment through the secretary, it's for two and a half weeks from now. We haven't got that kind of time. And fourth, even in this age of telecom, email, and Skype, nothing will ever beat real face-to-face contact. So it's senator Joe or bust! Come on."

We went to the Capitol Visitor Center, but it had closed for the day. I noticed two other police officers coming down from 1st Street and, thinking I had to get into the senate at all costs, I walked briskly up to the Capitol and made a bee line for the senate side. I didn't look behind me until I'd gotten close to the steps going up to the north wing. When I did look back I no longer saw Tyler, but there were now three police officers coming toward me from different directions. I headed under the steps into the passageway used for dropping off automobile passengers, and got to the door to the senate. But, peering inside the building, I saw four armed Capitol police officers rushing in my direction. I looked outside and saw two more coming from my left. This was not good. I ran out the right side of the passageway, and around the corner of the north wing.

I could hear footsteps getting closer and heard police car sirens coming up from Constitution Ave. The next sound I heard was a loud metallic clank, followed immediately by the feeling of something being thrown over my head. Everything went dark, and I was grabbed from behind and pulled backward. Quickly, I heard another metallic clank and all the outside noises disappeared.

24

I didn't know who was kidnapping me. It could have been checkers, a healed-up pentagram, Ted Turdington, Brian Warner.... No scenario was good, so I said the first thing that came to my mind: "I've got an annuity I'll sign over to you!"

"Careful. Watch your step. Stay with me," I heard a voice say in reply. I didn't recognize the owner of the voice; it was someone completely new. But it was a lispy and raspy voice, giving me the impression I'd been abducted by Harvey Fierstein. Then the man let out a horrible cough and hacked uncontrollably for several seconds.

"Who are you?" I asked.

"Not yet," he said.

It seemed like we were moving through narrow passages and the man held me close. We went down stairs and down ramps. The small canvass bag tied around my neck allowed me to breathe, but was too tight to easily remove and didn't allow me a peek at anything. We made several turns on our journey and it felt like we'd walked at least a quarter mile. Finally, we stopped.

I felt him loosen the bag and pull it from my head. Looking

at him, my first impression was that he didn't look like Harvey Fierstein. He was tall and solidly built—not quite overweight—and appeared somewhere in his 60s. Looking around the space, it was a very old and musty-looking concrete room about 15 feet square with two metal doors, no windows, and a ceiling about six and a half feet high. Other than that, it was very nicely decorated. There was a large area rug, three antique standing lamps, two overstuffed chairs, a chaise lounge, wall tapestries and paintings, and a plant hanging in one corner from the ceiling.

"Can I get you a pop?" he said.

"A frozen pop?"

"No, a Coke, something like that."

"Yeah, that would be great."

He let out another horrible cough as he got the soda out of a compact refrigerator. It was a deep, rumbling cough, that sounded like a box truck hitting a really big pothole. "That's caused by the niter," he said.

"What's niter?"

"Never mind. It's not niter. Have a seat." He handed me the Coke. "It's asbestos. You're in the tunnels underneath the Capitol."

"I didn't know there were tunnels under the Capitol."

"There are miles of tunnels under the Capitol. Utility tunnels, subway tunnels, pedestrian tunnels, railroad tunnels.... These things connect 23 buildings in the Capitol area. Where you're at now is my own private little hideaway, which is why I had to put the sack over your head. No one knows how to get here, and no one is going to know."

"Why is it so hot?"

"It's always this hot. I can usually keep it down to around 85 degrees. Maybe 80 if it's the end of January."

"Are you Artemus Schreckengost?"

He laughed. "Me? Artemus Schreckengost? No, that's not me."

"Do you know him? Is he a real person?"

"Yes, Artemus Schreckengost is a real person. No, I cannot tell you anything about him. Tell you anything else you want to know. Not that."

"Are you afraid of him?"

"Me, no. I don't care what happens. I'm going to die soon anyway. But I feel empathy for the rest of the human race, and I would feel bad if I helped it become extinct."

"That doesn't make any sense."

"Walk in my shoes. It'll make too much sense."

"So, who are you?"

"Nobody in particular. Just another walking-around American."

"But you know who gives the orders."

"No one gives orders."

"Nobody gives the orders to target a president?"

"No. Nobody gives any orders for specific missions. It's not set up that way. If somebody gave orders, then a direct link to that specific crime could be traced back to that individual. So it doesn't work that way."

"Then..."

"How does it work?"

"Yeah."

"Training. People are trained for the situation, not for the specific mission."

"But...."

"There was a Miami Oswald."

"What?"

"You have heard of Lee Harvey Oswald."

"Yes."

"The reason you have heard of Lee Harvey Oswald is because President Kennedy was killed in Dallas. Why Dallas? Not because Oswald was there. But because that is where every step in the process was allowed to run through to conclusion. It's the process that acts, not the people. You look confused."

"Um, yeah. A little."

"There was a Miami Oswald. Kennedy visited Miami a few days before Dallas. The process ran up its first few steps. All systems were go. Then the Secret Service got spooked and changed plans at the last minute. Kennedy flew out in a helicopter instead of going in a motorcade. No problem. The process immediately started churning in the next city. And now the world knows only Dallas and Lee Harvey Oswald, instead of Miami and James whatsisname."

"Dallas, Miami.... How many other cities had something like that?"

"You mean then or now?"

"How about now."

"There is one operator and one handler permanently stationed in each of the 25 largest cities in the United States. Plus a floating team consisting of five members that moves into position in a city if and when the process reaches that stage."

"And nobody gives them orders to do that?"

"Nobody issues any orders."

"How is that possible?"

"I told you, training. No one needs to tell you what to do. You are thoroughly trained to react in particular ways to each indicator as it occurs, like one of those automatic shuttle trains that has no driver. Based on the electronic indicators, the train knows what to do next. In our context, depending on the occurrence of various domestic social and political scenarios, as well as military and geopolitical events, each actor will automatically know what his next move should be."

"Sounds like a really good sales training conference," I said, trying to break the ice.

"Except salesmen don't typically go around assassinating heads of state."

"True. It's not a volume business."

"So if the process rises to the level," he continued, "where a crime will be committed, it has the appearance of being a localized event. It doesn't go beyond the person who is picked up for doing the deed."

"He won't talk?"

"No. Because he's incentivized in training. As I say, the training is very extensive. It includes a variety of methods in what you'd call brain washing. The police pick him up and for reasons that include psychological prohibitions, not to mention an absolute deniability on the part of those he might implicate, he won't tell the truth. The police have their man and it will go no further."

"They won't investigate the possibility of conspiracy?"

"Not in any way that seems like work, no. Police, FBI, prosecutors are like four-year-old children playing soccer. If you throw a ball on the field they'll all converge on the ball without thinking about what might be happening in other parts of the field. You are experiencing this yourself. Someone else shoots Greg Tousand and the police are all looking for you. They're devoting no resources to the possibility it was someone else."

"So who was Mr. Tousand?"

"A trainee. He was the Seattle Oswald back in the 80s. He requested reassignment and ended up over at the Air and Space Museum. But he had no children, divorced his wife, parents were dead, thereby lessening one of the incentives for keeping quiet. He was considered a tip risk and was closely watched. And he was taken care of rather artfully if you ask me."

This was amazing. For weeks I'd been trying to get someone to talk to me about what was going on. And at every turn I'd gotten nowhere. Now, all of a sudden, this man who'd either rescued or kidnapped me—depending on how this played out—was spilling the beans about their whole operation. I didn't know his motive, but I thought I should keep him talking while I could. "Why does it seem like all these government agencies are involved when one of these things happens?" I asked.

"Remember, you have to distinguish between before-the-fact conspiracy versus after-the-fact conspiracy. Before the fact, as I say, there are only the trainees and their automatic signals. The behavior you see exhibited by those agencies can largely be attributed to after-the-fact conspiracy. They all have something to hide, unrelated to the event itself, and they all have asses to cover. Imagine how you'd feel if you were in charge of the Secret Service or FBI and a president of the United States gets killed under your nose. These agencies go into a mad scramble to cover any evidence that might show they were negligent in their duties, naturally giving the appearance that they are part of some conspiracy."

"But there are moles in these agencies, aren't there?"

"Fewer than you might think. You see, there's no need. The behavior of law enforcement agencies and police departments is very predictable. They never deviate. And their learning curve is glacially slow. Every possible scenario on the part of law enforcement is run in training. It's funny; you'll see special units devoted to counter-terrorism or counter-espionage, but never to counter-revolution. No one is devoted to researching, investigating, and analyzing government-changing threats perpetrated by the most powerful interests within this country. The National Threat Assessment Center is fairly new and comes close to that type of thing, but they only keep track of lone nuts and hate groups. They're looking for outsiders. The insiders are left alone."

"Somebody who works there is one of them."

"Yeah, Tim Johnson. He makes sure the focus stays on outsiders. The insiders have to be allowed to continue as an additional check and balance on the system, in case the people make a mistake and elect the wrong individual."

"What about me? Where do I fit in?"

"You're a gnat flying into their ear. You're in the process of being swatted."

"Does the CIA run this?"

"No, the CIA does not run this. There are four trainers who operate the camp, and their day jobs are with the CIA. But they do this on their own time. There's no official connection to the agency."

"There's no central control? No 'Mr. Big'?"

"Oh, yes. There is a Mr. Big."

"Is that Artemus Schreckengost?"

"No. I told you, you won't get anything out of me about Artemus Schreckengost."

"Then who's Mr. Big?"

"You're so eager. Just settle down. He's William Bradford, the director of the Federal Interagency Committee for the Management of Noxious and Exotic Weeds."

This one caused me to pause. I dropped my cool exterior for a moment, saying, "Are you serious?"

"I kid you not. The committee coordinates the resources of over a dozen federal agencies to prevent and control the spread of unwanted invasive plant species. It's a primo appointment. The fucker. He got noxious weeds and I got this."

"What does he do there?"

"He runs the place like his own private fiefdom. The official work of the committee should cost no more than a million dollars a year. William has managed to run up a 17 million dollar annual budget. And not all of that money is going to manage exotic weeds, at least not the vegetable kind."

"So, if nobody gives orders, what's his job?"

"He sets the training parameters, manages post-event clean up, monitors and deflects any investigations that get too close to any previous or potential operation. There's getting to be quite a history to manage. William is the fifth Big since 1945. The second Mr. Big was, let's say, the most proactive. He ran the show from 1960 to 1975, and his training philosophy was a tad extreme, if you ask some people. It created a burdensome legacy that all future Bigs have had to manage."

"I've seen that guy, William Bradford. It has to be him. I watched a video that showed Major Brian Warner, that Tim Johnson from the Secret Service, and one other guy who was telling the others what to do."

"Yup, that was William. I L-M-A-O when I saw that video go up on the internet!"

"You sound like you enjoy this stuff."

"It is what it is. You either go along with it and find ways to laugh or you become a victim. And this boy learned long ago he didn't want to be a victim."

"What do you think about William?"

"For years I've been dying to tell William what I thought of him," he said with a laugh/cough. "But now, being a Christian woman, I can't say it!"

"So how does someone get to be Mr. Big?"

"The sitting Big selects someone, and the selection cannot be challenged. You see, I was in line to be the next Mr. Big back in 2005. I thought I was going to be a shoe-in, but then at the last minute I heard William had been picked instead of me."

"So you're still pissed off about it. Is that why you're telling me this?"

"Not so much pissed off as when I see an opportunity to have some fun, I take it. Maybe I'm just a passive-aggressive bitch, but I'll tell you almost everything I know and send you out of here to try to bring down the conspirators. I don't think you can do it, but you'll bug the shit out of William and the others trying. I hope you don't mind being here solely for my entertainment."

"Well, heck. If I can stop this from happening—and I think I can—and bring amusement to someone in the process, then that's more than I could ask for."

"Maybe with one shot in a million you'll succeed. Which would actually be alright with me, because I happen to like this president. But you didn't hear that from me."

"So who's the operator in DC? The one who's going to do the job coming up. Is it Todd Manderville?"

"I don't know the name of the DC operator. I've been out of the loop for a few years, and this is a need-to-know business, you understand."

"How did they kill John Dean?"

"John Dean? The Nixon administration's John Dean?"

"Yeah, he was killed by those people, wasn't he?"

"Why in heaven would anybody want to do anything to John Dean?"

"Are you saying Dean wasn't killed as a way to send a message?"

"Don't you think we have enough to do? People aren't

killed to send messages. They're killed because they're a direct threat to national destiny or to the success of operations. Eliminating someone can be done very efficiently. But it's still a lot of work—to both carry out and to manage thereafter. Even the second Mr. Big didn't go around offing people just to send messages. You've been reading too many political thrillers, Hank."

Here I got perturbed. One of the crown jewels of The Theory had just been shot down as casually as if it were a passenger pigeon, becoming extinct before my eyes. "Okay, what's really going on here? Why should I trust you? What 'automatic signal' is causing you to do this?"

"You're not a programmed indicator, Hank."

"You won't even tell me your name. So what should I call you? 'Deep Throat'?"

"For God's sake, don't call me 'Deep Throat'! Give me a small man any day."

"That's not the point!"

"Jesus Christ, Hank. I know what the point is, and giving you my name is only going to distract from the point. Now listen to me. I'll bet you heard the line about people being suckers for the truth. Well here's the line in the real world: Fundamentally, people are suckers for pornography; no one cares about the truth, Bubba. And I just hope you fall right on your ass!"

I felt the need to redirect the conversation. "You wanna buy some life insurance?" I said.

He laughed and then coughed horribly. "I've got an advanced case of asbestosis. I'd never pass the medical exam."

"Not a problem. If NALIC of Maryland denies an application, I'm allowed to act as a broker and get you coverage through any company that will accept you."

"So that means I'd get something like $10,000 of coverage

WILLIAM A. MAYS

and have to pay $1,000 every month for a premium."

"What does it matter to me? All I care about is my commission."

He looked at me for a moment. "Touché, my friend," he said. "Well played."

"So now that we understand each other, what can you help me with?"

"How about I tell you where the training camp is? It's located at a place you're quite familiar with. The Hunting Hill Quarry."

"Hunting Hill Quarry?"

"It's underground, under the front part where the main buildings are."

"You don't say."

"The quarry was perfect. If anyone sees huge volumes of dirt and rock being excavated out of a quarry, who's going to question it?"

"Thanks, that is helpful."

"I'll do you one better. How would you like to get an appointment to see William Bradford?"

"I would like that."

He picked up a phone, hit a speed-dial button, and got a secretary. "Molly, does William have any appointment slots open tomorrow?" .... "Uh huh." .... "Okay. Hold on." He hit the mute button and told me, "The whole board is having a meeting tomorrow afternoon. God knows why the Friday before a three-day weekend. But how would you like to give a presentation to the board?"

Seminars were a gift from God to insurance agents. I jumped at the chance.

"Molly," he said into the phone, "put Mr. Hank Stafford

174

down for a twenty-minute presentation during tomorrow's board meeting." .... "That's it. Thank you."

I couldn't believe it. In the space of an hour this guy had saved me from the cops, exposed the assassination organization, and become a center of influence for my financial services business. The people he was referring me to may have been cold-hearted killers, but even they needed solid family financial plans. And though he was willing to only go so far in bringing this thing down —and was sure it wasn't far enough for me to actually succeed—I still had an ace up my sleeve: Amber's plan to kill Todd.

"You've had quite a day," he said. "You must be tired."

"Yeah, I'm pretty beat."

"Well, you can't stay here." He had me get up, put the bag back over my head, and took me through the tunnels to a room near the Capitol South metro stop. "You'll be safe here," he said. "Tomorrow morning just walk through that door and you'll be on the eastbound platform."

"Thanks," I said. "I'll let you know how everything goes."

He coughed and laughed. As he left the room I listened to the sound of the cough/laugh fade down the tunnel.

25

The first order of business the next morning was placing a call to Debbie Poindexter. Debbie was the OSHA employee who'd first referred Amber my way. This time, I felt she could help me with a little information on our Capitol-tunnel friend. I explained to her I'd gotten a referral to someone who clearly needed life, health, disability, or long-term-care insurance or some combination thereof, but the referring person had forgotten his name and, even though I'd spoken to him myself, I'd misplaced his number. I said he seemed to be in his 60s and was probably from the Midwest.

"How do you know he's from the Midwest," Debbie asked.

"Based on his accent and the fact that he said 'pop' instead of 'soda' and 'sack' instead of 'bag'. I'm guessing downstate Illinois, Iowa or Nebraska."

"Okay," she said, "We have an extensive file on the Capitol tunnels, but I can only give you what's already in the public record." She checked and called back later, saying "There was quite a serious asbestos problem down there that the Architect of the Capitol is in the process of having abated. The workers filed complaints over health effects and the only person I see that could be a match for you is Robert Livingstone. He's 58 and was born in Moline, Illinois."

"Can you tell me his job and how long he's worked there?"

"He's a supervisor. Been there since December 1992."

That sounded like my guy. I was about to hang up with Debbie when she said in a somewhat worried, hesitant voice "Oh, Hank, by the way. John Poindexter called me the other day."

"He's related to you, isn't he? That's not unusual."

"Distant relative. I only met him once, and he's never called me before."

This was the relative who'd been involved in Iran-Contra and had directed a government program that predicted the odds of future assassinations. "What did he want?" I asked.

"This is what reminded me," she said. "He was asking about Robert Livingstone too."

My heart stopped. What were these people up to? "Did he say why he needed the information?"

"No."

Another wave of paranoia swept over me. And time was getting short. There were too many variables and too many things that could go wrong. I felt like I had to make a decision regarding Amber's plan. Today was the day she'd wanted to carry it out. And based on everything I'd discovered to date, everything I'd learned from Amber, from Todd, from Private Huguenot, from Special Agent Turdington, from Tyler, from Major Warner, and especially from Robert Livingstone, I concluded that Todd had to be the DC operator. To save the life of the current president of the United States, Todd Manderville must die. There was no time left to try to figure out who might be lying or who might be an impostor.

I took the train to Wheaton and walked to Amber's school.

I knew her classroom was somewhere on the first floor and I went around the building till I found it. Peering in the window, I watched Amber work her class of fourth graders. One of the kids noticed me fogging up the window and he got Amber's attention. I motioned for her to come out and she left the class in charge of an aid. Out in the schoolyard by the swings I stuttered out my tortured decision. "I told you to wait until you heard from me, right?" I started. "Well, now you're hearing from me. I think you should go ahead with what you wanted to do."

Amber was calm, cool, at ease, and spoke as if my urgent, borderline-frantic tone confused her. "I didn't need you to tell me that, Hank. I was going to do it anyway. I've already got the antifreeze poured into his Gatorade bottles."

"Geez," I said, covering my internal tumult with nonchalance, "it's great to see you're not at all disturbed by any of this."

"It has to get done, Hank. And I haven't forgotten the promise I made to you. I sent in the form last week."

"What form?"

"The change of beneficiary form. So that you can get your million dollars."

Shock mingled with disbelief. "Amber, did you send a change of beneficiary form to NALIC with my name on it?"

"Of course. I put you down to get 20 percent of the money, which is a million like I said. How else were you going to get it?"

My brain felt like it was imploding. The appearance of impropriety in this case had already reached outrageous levels. Putting as a beneficiary the agent who sold her a policy on the life of a husband she was about to murder not only sent that appearance into the stratosphere, it propelled it all the way to Pluto. I wasn't insisting on getting any money, but felt if Amber wanted to give me some of the proceeds after she'd received them then that would have been okay. I'd been running in my head everything from gift-tax considerations to how to open Swiss bank accounts in anticipation of the possibility. But now I felt like I was standing on the first floor of the tallest house of cards on earth, as it was about to collapse. I almost started begging Amber to not go through with it, but if she didn't then one of the country's most capable presidents in generations was going to die.

"Why do you look like that?" she said. "What are you thinking?"

"Nothing," I said. "Nothing, Amber. I've just decided that I'm going to sacrifice myself for my country. Go do what you need to do, and I guess I'll see you around."

"You know something, Hank? I wish I could give you a blowjob on this swing set."

"You know something, Amber? I don't think even that would distract me from what's on my mind."

"You worry too much," she said, and planted a big, wet kiss on my mouth. "I have to get back to my classroom."

I wandered aimlessly back to the Metro station. I didn't know what street I was on, but I looked to my right into the parking lot of a 7-Eleven and thought I saw Tyler's car. A closer look produced a positive identification and I went inside. Sure enough, there was Tyler putting a veggie burrito into the microwave. I asked what had happened to him the previous evening after we'd been separated.

"I got picked up by the cops," he said. "But don't worry, dude; I covered for you."

"So you didn't tell them about me?"

"All I did was tell them your name and where you work."

If this was covering for me, I thought, what could ratting me out look like?

"I didn't tell them," Tyler continued, "that you shot that guy at the museum."

"I didn't shoot the guy at the museum."

"But that's what they wanted to hear. And I didn't give them what they wanted."

"They asked you about that?"

"No, but I could tell they would have loved to hear that."

Between Tyler and Amber, I was having my doubts whether I could ever trust reality again. "Tyler, you're the man," is all I could think to say. He'd been questioned without being charged, but they did tell his father he and another man had been acting in a suspicious manner in the vicinity of the Capitol. Tyler said his dad had taken today off, and that gave me an idea. "I'd like to meet your father," I told him. I decided seeing him at his home was probably safer than going back to FBI headquarters, and if I could judge where he stood on all this I could perhaps bring him in as an ally.

Tyler had been staying at his parents' house since his place got ransacked. "My dad's cool," he said as we pulled in the driveway. "He smoked weed back in the 70s."

"That doesn't mean anything," I replied. "Everyone smoked weed back in the 70s. There are people who had hair down to the middle of the backs and got high at Black Sabbath concerts back in the 70s who are now members of the Heritage Foundation and read the Weekly Standard."

"Sucks for them," Tyler said. "But my dad's alright."

We went in the house and Tyler introduced me as the guy he tried to "bum rush the Capitol" with. Feeling the need to counter with a more clean-cut representation of myself, I said I was "Hank Stafford of the National American Life Insurance Company of Maryland," and presented Mr. Delony with my business card.

"Come in, Hank. Have a seat."

The elder Delony seemed pleasant, offering me a choice of water or soda. Then he asked what the purpose was of our venture to the Capitol, and I replied I had information I thought would be of interest to the chairman of the Senate Homeland Security Committee.

"Well, I work for the FBI," he replied back. "Perhaps you could trust me with whatever information you have."

Ay, there was the rub. In spite of Tyler's belief in a conspiracy yet insistence that his father was an upstanding guy, I balked. At this point I had very little trust left. I had to find out where Mr. Delony really stood. "Sir," I said, "I appreciate your interest in what I know. But I was wondering if I might first ask you what you know."

"Alright," he said, "but let me ask you a question first. Were you at the National Air and Space Museum yesterday?"

"Now I'm going to ask you a question. Is there an agent who works at the FBI named Theodore Turdington?"

"Are you going to answer my question, Hank?"

"I will answer your question by asking have you heard the name Susan Underhill?"

"How is that name important to you?"

"Are you saying it's not important to you?"

"Does this have anything to do with the museum?"

"Would I mention the name if it didn't?"

"So are you saying you were at the museum?"

"Is that what I said?"

"How is it that you match the description of someone who was there yesterday?"

"Did something happen there?"

"You don't know?"

"Did I say I didn't?"

"What do you know?"

"Would Tim Johnson, Major Brian Warner, or William Bradford of Exotic Weeds also like to know what I know?"

"Why are you avoiding the subject?"

"How is Hunting Hill Quarry avoiding the subject?"

"Hunting Hill Quarry?"

"Did I let that slip out?"

"What are you hiding?"

"Can you tell me if you're familiar with the case of Julia Scheider?"

"You mean Peggy's daughter?"

"You know her?"

"Doesn't everyone in law enforcement know Peggy Scheider by now?"

"What's the status of the case?"

"Why do you want to know?"

"Would it interest you to know that I'm friends with Julia Scheider?"

"Why would it interest me?"

"If I had that answer would I be asking all these questions?"

"Hank, why aren't you taking this seriously?"

"Isn't this funny?"

"Am I laughing?"

"Are you involved in a plot to assassinate President Obama?"

"Are you crazy?"

"Do I look crazy?"

"Tyler, leave the room."

The elder Delony abruptly put a halt to our bloodless

parrying by ordering his son out of the room. I didn't know what was about to happen, but considering what had happened up till now, I half expected horns to sprout from the man's head. Instead, I got the heart-felt lecture of a concerned father.

"Hank, I love my son," he started. "For 20 years I've nurtured him and watched him grow. It hasn't always been easy. It's been a lot of work. But that's the responsibility that is automatically yours when you have a child. Maybe there were things I would rather have been doing or people I would rather have been hanging around with. But taking proper care to raise a child is just something you've got to do. It is not negotiable. I've got a huge amount of my time, energy, and mental and physical resources invested in that boy, Hank. And now, 20 years later, maybe I can't stand his music, but I know he doesn't do drugs or hang out with criminals, and I know that at heart he's a good and decent person. And that he's going to be okay in this world partly because I chose to do what was right by him years ago instead of maybe what I would rather have been doing at the time. I sacrificed, but I don't regret a moment of it. So I'm going to ask you one more question. Do you want to throw away 20 years of my sacrifice?"

I had no answer.

"If you don't realize it," he continued, "then let me spell it out for you: what you are doing with my son could get him killed. You are involved in something that is way beyond Tyler's control, but what's worse is it's something way beyond your control. And you are taking him right down with you." He leaned in closer. "What I'm telling you to do is stop it. Stop getting my son into this."

"Well, technically, he was the one who...."

"I know he's an adult and can make his own decisions. But if I see a train wreck coming, I'm going to by God pull him off the tracks if it's within my power to do so. Please, Hank. Leave my son out of this."

26

I'd left the Delony home not only without an additional ally, but possibly with one fewer than I had when I went in. As disappointing as the notion was, I had no time to think about it. I had an insurance seminar to give at Noxious Weeds in a couple hours and I had to get to the office in Beltsville to pick up my materials.

I got off the bus and walked to the office cursing the fact that my best suit had been swiped by some kid at the other 7-Eleven. Business casual was not the way I wanted to go in to a sales meeting with federal bigwigs, or with the arch fiend behind a violent overthrow of the United States government.

No sooner had I tried to find room in my planner for a lightning-fast trip to the Men's Wearhouse, a pickup truck squealed to a halt on the other side of Baltimore Ave. I saw the driver stare at me intently before he hit the gas and laid a patch on a U-turn across four lanes of traffic to my side of the street. Under normal circumstances this might tend to bring a person to a heightened alertness. Under my circumstances it made me decide to run like hell. The truck paced me as I bolted down the sidewalk looking for a place to duck in. Then I heard a voice. "Hey, I want my 20 dollars!"

I looked and suddenly recognized the person as the kid I'd sent to the motel to get my bags. He explained he'd gone to my room, gotten the bags and put them in his truck. But when he'd come back to the 7-Eleven he didn't see me. With no time to argue about why it took him more than a half hour to get back, I gave him the $20—plus $10 for the beer I failed to buy him—took my bags, and continued on my way. The fortuitous coincidence of getting my suit back right before the big meeting gave a boost to my recently sagging optimism. "This must be my lucky day," I said as I headed into NALIC's office on Baltimore Ave.

Going there, of course, was a risk. The police—and God knows who else—were looking for me and knew where I worked. But I was a salesman who'd just been handed a group of good leads. I was going to do what I did best, as best as I could, come hell or high water. And that meant collecting my laptop—which contained my Powerpoint presentation—NALIC information sheets, contact cards, maybe the NALIC table banner, and anything else I could think of to maximize the chances of audience members taking the next step.

I walked briskly through the building, went up the stairs instead of elevator, snuck past reception, and got to my office, essentially an eight foot by six foot closet filled with clutter and mess. This was the reason I preferred to meet clients in the conference room instead of in my office. The artifice of professional opulence would have come crashing down once a client saw where his financial services representative called home.

Only in my third year with NALIC, I'd done well enough to at least move up from a cubicle to an office. But Million Dollar Round Table status was what really guaranteed you a set of nice digs that you would feel good showing to a client. I'd come so close the previous year I could taste it, but I'd lost one of my best clients toward the end of the year when his office was raided by federal agents and his boss was arrested. The poor fellow lost his job as a result and, without income, had to let his policy lapse. Thus are the fortunes of being an insurance agent. You take the bad with the good.

I changed into my suit, collected my materials, and was just about to leave when I felt a presence at my office door. I turned around to see Rich Fox with a concerned look on his face. "Hank," he said, "it's nice of you to stop by."

The man had a sixth sense. I could have been invisible and he would know I was there. "Hi, Rich. I've got a big presentation to do at a federal agency. It could be big."

"I hope so, Hank. Because that's what I wanted to talk to you about." He came in and closed the door. "You haven't been around much lately. I know you're just about an established agent, so how you go about your business is getting to be up to you. But I'm beginning to see warning signals."

"What signals are those, Rich?"

"I've been around long enough to know that when an agent starts to change his habits and routine, it almost always indicates trouble ahead. And sure enough, your number of submitted apps the past couple weeks has gone way down. It's not showing yet in your paid-cases rate, but that's just due to the lag time. Your bottom-line production is about to take a serious hit, Hank."

"Rich, you've got to give me some time. I've been working some really big centers of influence in the federal government. And they're about to pay off big. I've got my first seminar at a big agency one hour from now."

"What's the agency?"

"The Federal Interagency Committee for the Management of Noxious and Exotic Weeds."

I'd never seen Richard W. Fox speechless before. But it was happening now.

"There are some really important people in there," I explained, "and I'm presenting to them today."

"Production, Hank. That's all I care about. You know that. You're a good agent; there's nothing more I can tell you. You know how it's done. All I want to see is production, production, production."

"This could be big, Rich."

"Alright, Hank. I've said my piece. I'll let you have at it." Rich opened the door. "Oh, by the way," he said. "Someone from the FBI was here looking for you. His name was Turgidson or something. He wanted to question you about an attempted murder."

"Really?" I said. "That's strange. I wonder if he was looking for the right person."

"Right. And that reminds me. The DC police were also here looking for you. This was about an actual murder."

"Boy, they must really have things mixed up."

"Wait, there's one more thing." He closed the door again. "I got a call from the home office about you. It seems one of your clients has put you down as a beneficiary on her policy. Do you know anything about that?"

"Really? Which one?"

"Amber Manderville."

"Hmm, that's interesting. I'll give her a call and see if I can find out what she's up to."

"That's fine, Hank. But..." He paused, searching for the right words. "Don't raise too much concern with her. We need to keep her as a client."

"I'll tread carefully, Rich."

"Good man." He opened the door and started down the hall, saying to himself, "Mr. Production. Hank 'Production' Stafford...."

27

The address I'd gotten from Robert Livingstone, 1620 L Street, was a 12-story office building less than a half mile from the White House and a block from the Washington Post. Venturing inside, I presented myself to the security desk. The woman in charge had me sign in, made a call, gave me a pass sticker, and told me to take the elevator to the 11th floor.

Going up the elevator, I noticed on the button panel only the 11th and 12th floors had locks next to them. Currently the 11th was not locked, and the doors opened onto a spectacular room. It appeared to be the reception area, but was so huge it must have taken up fully a third of the floor's entire square footage. There was a ton of open space, statues, wall hangings, even a fountain. The floor was marble and the furnishings appeared to be mahogany. I went to the receptionist and introduced myself. "How much space does the committee have in this building?" I asked.

"We take up all of the top two floors," she replied.

"Wow," I said, looking around. "Not bad for a little agency like Weeds."

"We do important work," she said. "The meeting just

started. You can go on up."

There was a wide staircase behind the receptionist that went up to the 12th floor. I ascended and at the top saw a set of large wooden double doors. Turning the brass knob, I went in and beheld another huge room as opulently decorated as the one I'd just left. In the center was a gigantic conference table surrounded by 30 chairs. They were not all full; only 11 people were currently in the room. But the place had a knights-of-the-round-table feel to it.

I sat in a chair at the side of the room and observed the proceedings. A man was talking about the minutes of the last meeting and old business. Then someone noticed me sitting there and asked if I could introduce myself. I gave my name and affiliation, and then another man piped up.

"Yes, welcome, Mr. Stafford. We're expecting you. Though I thought you would have been delayed at the office."

"No, always on time," I said. "No such thing as early, just late and on time."

"That's very nice," he said. "We're going to take care of some old business and then we'll get right to you. I'm William Bradford, chairman of the committee." Bradford was a sharp-looking man in a three-piece suit, his graying hair gelled up into a pompadour.

"Very nice to meet you, sir," I said.

The committee continued on with its business. I sat there and listened to lengthy discussions about biopesticides, invasive prediction parameters, onionweed eradication, the development of a weed factbook, and the issuing of healthy habitats awards. My eyelids began to feel like 16-ton weights and I wrestled to remain conscious. Suddenly, William Bradford called out, "Mr. Stafford, thank you for waiting. I think we're ready for your presentation now."

I asked where I could plug in my laptop and was told there were six projectors around the room to choose from. "This is a beautiful table," I said. "What's it made of?"

"Brazilian rosewood," came the reply. I could see where some of that $17 million budget Robert Livingstone referred to was going. And I'd bet they didn't have any asbestos up there either. I got everything set up and then started the show.

I had a stack of $10 bills and passed one around to each person at the table. "If I don't have a good idea, you can keep the money," I said. "Does everyone here have a family? Spouse? Children? Maybe even grandchildren or parents who might depend on you? How many here are the main breadwinners for your families? Do some or all of you have mortgages? College expenses for the kids to consider? A nice retirement to plan for? A flow of income to maintain? Now, how many of you would like your spouse to lose your home or not have enough money for old age? How many would like your children to have to skip going to college? Some of you might have good-sized estates. How will your surviving family members come up with the money to pay estate taxes should something happen to you? Some of you might have thought you were going to meet a life insurance salesman today. Turns out you were misinformed. I don't sell life insurance. I sell a college education for daddy and mommy's little boy and girl; I sell homes where children play happily in the front yard, and flowers bloom in the back; I sell self-respect to old men, but I sell it to them when they are young. I sell peace of mind when it's time to pass your estate on to your heirs. It's true that doing something costs something. But doing nothing also costs something. And quite often, it costs a lot more. The bottom line is all of you folks will have the same problems when I walk out as you had when I walked in. I'm asking that when I walk out, you let me take your problems with me."

I ran the slide show, which illustrated NALIC's longevity, financial strength, and wide range of products. I talked a little about business, personal, and estate planning in relation to various insurance, savings, and investment products. I spoke of protecting and building assets to guarantee retirement, pay off mortgages, pay for college, and maintain income in case of financial disruption, including the potential need for long-term care in old age. I pointed out the tax-free accumulation benefits of permanent life insurance and annuities, and illustrated the high guaranteed cash values of NALIC's permanent policies in later years. I kept asking questions to keep people interested, e.g., "Is anyone here paying extra money or thinking of paying extra money toward your mortgage to get it paid off sooner?" This led to a discussion of life insurance as a more cost effective way to accomplish that goal while providing a lump sum to pay off the mortgage immediately if the breadwinner should die. I thought the seminar was going very well. Then William Bradford spoke up.

"You've said there's almost nothing life insurance can't do. But can life insurance assure life? Can it guarantee someone living past the time when they were supposed to die?"

"Life insurance is a marvelous tool, Mr. Bradford. But its powers unfortunately are limited to the realm of financial security. One needs to use other methods to prolong life."

"I have an idea of some of those methods, Mr. Stafford. What are some of the methods you would use?"

"I would recommend keeping a very close eye on the things that pose the greatest threat."

"And if you discover a threat?"

"I do everything in my power to expose it and remedy it."

"Do you ever give up pursuing what you think might be

right, if there's enough money involved?"

"Never. I do what's right for my clients regardless of the money that could be made. What I offer is protection and peace of mind to everyone from the restaurant dishwasher all the way up to the most important person in the land. It's called mission before commission. The service I provide is too important to corrupt for personal gain."

"You're a very stubborn person, Mr. Stafford."

"Not stubborn, just committed to the system and ideals that our founders fought a revolution over."

"Well, there's idealism and then there's reality. And those who can't accept reality usually come to a very unexpected end."

"Then it's a good thing I have lots of NALIC life insurance, Mr. Bradford! Thank you for the question."

"I've got some important assets I would like preserved and protected, Mr. Stafford. I do hope you'll stay after the meeting and we can get more personal."

"I was planning on it."

The questions from the other bureaucrats tended to be less cryptic and more directly related to financial services. At the end of the presentation, five of them filled out my contact cards requesting further information, and eight of them gave me the $10 bill back—Bradford not being one of them. When the committee's official business concluded, I spoke with folks individually and set two appointments there on the spot. Then William Bradford asked me to come back to his office.

We walked through a sconce-lined hallway with wall-to-wall oriental carpeting. At the end, Bradford placed his thumb on a print reader and opened a heavy wooden door. We walked in, he closed the door and said, "Most likely, Mr. Stafford, you won't be leaving this building alive."

"Who's Artemus Schreckengost?" I asked.

"I'm just wondering, with all the trouble you're in," he said as we sat at his desk, "why you chose to come here. Did you think I would just let you leave?"

"You have to let me leave. Two of your committee members just made appointments with me to review their families' financial health."

"It's your physical health you should be worried about."

"I know something that would be of great interest to you. If you let me go I'll tell you what it is."

"What you know is not important to me. But it would be much healthier for you to just take a bribe."

"Mr. Bradford," I said, looking at my watch, "right now your little plan is in the process of being squashed. And I'm going to make a million dollars in the process. I don't need your bribe."

"You seem very confident for someone who doesn't know what he's talking about."

"If I don't know, then let me go."

"I'd like to play something for you that might bring things into perspective." He pushed a button on his desk and sound emitted from speakers surrounding the room.

In quadraphonic clarity the recording said: "How are you about unprotected sex?" "I'm okay with it. I'm on the pill." Some bumping, breathing, and squeaking followed.

"Sound familiar?" said Bradford. "I'll fast forward a little. But just a bit. It doesn't take long."

The recording continued: "Has Todd told you anything else about his mission or the plot?" "Nothing. I don't know any more than what I told you." "How can you be so sure that Todd will actually be caught up in this assassination?" "Everything, and I mean everything Todd has ever told me has been the truth. If he says something is going to happen, then it happens. That's why I got so freaked out. Todd said he'd probably be killed doing this thing. You don't know Todd, but he never guesses. If he says 'probably' he means 'definitely.'"

I said, "I didn't know the Federal Interagency Committee for the Management of Noxious and Exotic Weeds was involved in the proliferation of pornography. It seems like something the FBI might be interested in."

"Very funny, Mr. Stafford. I appreciate the gallows humor. But when you were discussing postcoitally with Mrs. Manderville some kind of assassination plot...."

"That wasn't me," I interrupted.

"Excuse me?"

"Are you saying that's me on that recording? Ha! I wish. She sounds hot. Who is that really?"

"Should I just have you killed now?"

"If it were up to me?"

"I do wish it didn't have to come to this. I actually like you a little. But I can't have you being a Canada goose flying into the engine of our airliner."

"A goose?"

"Bird strike, Mr. Stafford. Bird strike. It brings down airliners that are doing nothing more than simply keeping to their appointed schedules. Along comes a goose or flock of geese, stupidly bubbling into the path of the jumbo jet, and bang. There goes an engine. It puts the entire aircraft at risk."

"Well, your airliner is about to crash and it has nothing to do with me. But I can place a call and stop that from happening."

"You're a bubbling goose, Mr. Stafford. And this meeting is over." Bradford pushed another button on his desk. I heard the door unlatch. I instantly grabbed my laptop and NALIC materials, and bolted.

"Grab him!" Bradford yelled as the door swung wide, revealing checkers and pentagram on the other side. Not slowing down an iota, I shot past them before they had a chance to react. Running down the long hallway—NALIC information sheets fluttering in my wake—I looked back to see checkers giving chase, but pentagram only limping.

The door back to where I'd come from was locked. So with checkers gaining I went down a side hallway and found a stairwell. Once inside I had the bright idea of going up the stairs because they'd be expecting me to go down. Up I went and exited out onto the roof. At that point I decided maybe it wasn't such a bright idea after all. Where was I to go from there?

A connector went over to the building next door, so I ran across. But again I found myself in the same predicament. The doors leading inside were all locked and I had no place to go. Suddenly, I felt something hit the right shoulder pad of my suit jacket followed instantly by the sound of a loud pop. I looked around to see checkers shooting at me. I ran three quick steps and jumped off the two-story setback that sat on top of this building. I figured a broken leg would be preferable to being riddled with bullets.

I landed as straight as I could, tucking myself in at impact. The wind was severely knocked out of me, but I got up and didn't notice any serious breaks. Picking up my laptop, I hustled around the corner of the setback. There I saw a piece of air conditioning machinery that had seen better days. It was coming loose from its moorings, and I pulled it enough to reveal a ventilation duct. Just big enough for someone my size to fit into, I went in and pulled the machinery back as best I could with my feet.

Feeling my way through the duct in the dark, I pulled myself along until I noticed a grate with light coming through. I peeked into a room and it appeared to be empty. So I pushed the grate out and pulled a contortion routine snaking myself into the room. Once in, I stood on a chair and was just putting the grate back up when a man came in. "Hello," he said.

I gave the grate a hit with my fist and turned around. "Hi, how're you doing?" I said, hopping off the chair.

"Do I know you?" the man said.

"Not yet," I replied. "I'm here doing a seminar on life insurance and financial services." I was filthy, disheveled, my suit was ripped, but I still had my trusty, if battered, laptop at my side. I reached into my pocket and handed the man my business card. "Give me a call sometime," I said before patting him on the arm and making my exit.

I hustled to an elevator and then out the front of the building, trying to mingle in with a group of people. After walking a block to the Farragut North station on Connecticut Ave, I was on a train and out of there.

28

As I rode the Red Line I tried to think of a place to go. My last motel room was out of the question, and I wasn't sure I wanted to get another. This was getting very expensive, and as Rich Fox pointed out, I was about to hit a dry spell with my income. Then I thought of Julia's place. After a week of her being missing, I doubted anyone would be surveilling the place. I knew where she kept her extra key, and if I could slip in, I could keep the lights off and activity down, and I'd be safe.

After switching to the bus at Greenbelt, I got off in Julia's neighborhood in Calverton. The key to her place was under a little Buddha statue by the back door. I got in, closed the door behind me, and finally felt safe. Her place smelled like patchouli and looked lived in—a few dishes were out, books, magazines, and a few articles of clothing lay around.

I used my cell phone to check messages, and, trying the office first, got a recorded message saying the line was temporarily out of service. That had never happened before, but I went ahead and tried checking my home messages. Just as I started listening to the first one from Peggy, the call-waiting signal went off. It was

Tyler calling from his parents' phone.

"Dude," he said, "do you know what happened?"

"What happened with what?"

"Ah, you don't know? Dude, your office blew up!"

"What?! What do you mean 'blew up.' What happened?"

"I saw it on the news. There was a big explosion at the National American Life Insurance office in Beltsville."

"Holy shit." I didn't know what exactly happened, but I had an idea the kid from the 7-Eleven had probably returned my bags with something more than just my clothing and toiletries inside. And I'd bet someone met him at the motel and offered more than just 20 bucks and a six-pack of beer to bring the bags back to me and keep quiet. That must've been why it took him so long. These people were getting more and more serious. "Did they say anything about injuries?" I asked.

"No, they said there were no injuries."

I was relieved. It helped to a) have a shoebox office all the way on the other side of the floor from Rich's office and the administrative offices, and b) be in a business where the less time you spent in your office the more it showed you were working. My neighboring agents were likely out in the field.

"Dude, so what are you gonna do now?"

I was pissed and more determined than ever to expose these people. "I'm gonna buy a disposable camera," I said, "and go to the camp where they train their assassins and take lots of pictures."

"An assassin training camp? Awesome!" said Tyler. "I want to come."

"Tyler, your dad doesn't want you hanging around with me anymore."

"I know, dude. But damn, how many once in a lifetime chances do you get?"

"I would say one, Tyler."

"Hella straight!"

The next morning I took the bus to Wheaton. Tyler picked me up at the 7-Eleven and we headed toward Rockville. It was Saturday and I figured the quarry would not be operating. We'd be able to sneak in and look around to our hearts' content. We parked out on Piney Meetinghouse Road and walked up the road into the quarry. We were walking past the little office building where I'd had my conversations with Jim the employee, when I heard someone yell out, "Waydamin, hon. Yeu cana gudun thayer."

I turned around and, sure enough, it was Jim, standing on the building's stoop. I went up to him saying, "Jim, how are you doing? I didn't expect to see you here on a Saturday."

"Ahm gitinnin sum eou tee. Jess finnish mah breffist." Here he let out a belch so loud it echoed against the quarry rocks. "Wut kyin ah do fer yeu."

"You remember me, don't you? The private investigator? I got another very important lead and...."

"Yep, ah member yeu. Yur rennal kumnee nun teu happee wit yeu."

"Jim, I gotta ask you a favor. This is Marcus Jorgenson," I said, indicating Tyler. "He's a witness to a murder and we think one of the perpetrators may be hiding out here."

Jim raised his hands. "Ah dun wanna heer bout yur persnal prahbums. Yeu look rahn muchas ya lahk. Jess dun leave nah crush veekuls bahahn this tahm."

"You got it."

There were four other small buildings in the immediate area, and then the vast quarry beyond them. "I don't know," I said to Tyler. "If you were hiding a training camp where would you put the entrance?"

"A secret door inside one of these buildings."

"You think so?"

"Definitely."

We checked and found three of the buildings locked. Looking through the windows didn't reveal anything of interest. The fourth building was unlocked, but contained just mining equipment and a concrete floor. There was no possibility of a secret entrance. We walked past the buildings to the edge of the quarry's boundary with the adjacent neighborhood. As I looked out into the vastness—the quarry had to cover half a square mile—I said, "This is a needle in a haystack." Then I looked to my right, through the trees into the neighborhood on the other side. A road came to a dead end at the tree line, and there was a building there that did not look residential. "If there were covert operations going on here, don't you think the quarry employees would wonder who were all these people going back and forth? I mean look at Jim. I couldn't sneak by him."

Tyler nodded.

"But if I got in through a private road next door...." I kept looking at the area. After a minute, a car with Virginia plates pulled to the end of the road. Two men wearing business suits got out and walked into the small commercial structure. Tyler and I looked at each other.

We climbed into the tree line, through a ditch, and came out into the parking area. Carefully approaching the building, we looked in. It was essentially empty; there were certainly no people inside.

"They didn't just disappear, dude."

I turned the doorknob and it was unlocked. Once inside, we were looking around when Tyler yelped, "I found it!"

"Shhh, quiet." But there it was. A metal door in the floor. I carefully pulled it up about an inch and peeked inside. There was nothing but darkness. I opened it up the rest of the way and revealed a set of stairs. "What do you think?" I said.

"Let's go," said Tyler.

We walked down the steps, which went down about 10 feet below the floor, and came to another door. This door was vertical and, upon opening, revealed a long, lighted hallway. I instructed Tyler to close the door at the top of the stairs, and began cautiously to stick my head into the hallway when all of a sudden a loud metallic bang crashed through my ears. I jumped back like a frightened cat and pulled the door shut. Then I heard "Sorry, dude" from up the stairs.

"Please be careful," I said. Collecting myself, I reopened the door. The hallway was going in the right direction—back toward the quarry.

"What do we do if someone sees us?" asked Tyler.

"Run," I said as I got my camera out.

"How about we pretend we're one of them?"

I stopped walking. "What are you saying?"

"This is where they train recruits, right? So let's be their newest recruits."

The idea was so audacious it just might work. "Okay," I said. "We'll use the same name for you, Marcus Jorgenson. And I'll be...."

"Oswald Ray Bremer the third."

"What? No. Come on, we don't want to be obvious. I'll be Dirk Muncie."

"Oh, that's much better," Tyler said sarcastically. But it didn't matter; we were set.

The hallway ran about 60 yards, ending at another door. Slowly I opened it. Inside was what appeared to be a classroom.

Tyler saw a door on the other side of the room and headed for it. "Wait a minute," I said. "Look at this. Do you know what that is?"

"No, what is it?" said Tyler.

I held up what I'd found. "That is Randy Rabbit," I said. It looked like a collection of storyboards for a new Randy Rabbit cartoon.

"Is that what that major from the Pentagon...."

"Yep," I said. This time, Randy seemed to be the head of state. The storyboards showed him doing very repetitive activities. He leaves his house, gets into a car, rides along a route, goes into a venue, makes a speech, leaves the venue, rides along a route, gets out of his car, goes into the house. This routine repeats four times. Every time, the car is parked the exact same way, the movements to and from the car and the venues are exactly alike. The fifth time through the sequence, Randy is shot in the head as he's going into a venue. I put down the storyboards and started taking pictures.

"Hey, Hank. Take a look at this." Tyler had cracked open the door on the other side of the room. I went over and he opened it a little wider so I could see. What I saw was astounding: a giant, cavernous underground room that could have held two football fields, with a ceiling at least 15 feet high.

"Do you know when this quarry opened?" I asked Tyler as I snapped more pictures. "1955. Take a good look. This is where Lee Harvey Oswald, James Earl Ray, Sirhan Sirhan, Arthur Bremer, and dozens of others you never heard of got their training."

"It's the mother lode of mayhem," added Tyler.

"Let's go in." Once inside the huge room we walked along the wall. There was a group of about 12 people on the other side who hadn't noticed us yet. I took a couple more pictures. Then two people broke from the group and started across the room toward us. I put the camera away. "Come on, let's act like we belong here,"

I said. We strolled nonchalantly toward the group. The two men continued to approach us. The room was so big it felt as if we were walking toward each other for five minutes. When we got within reasonable vocal distance, I said, "Hi, we're here for the training."

"What as?" one of the men asked.

"What as? Well, we're trainees. We want to get trained."

"I see. So what's your names?"

"I'm Dirk Muncie."

"And I'm Tyler... Jorgenson."

"Good," said the man. "Come with us."

"Can I ask your names?" I said.

"Uh uh, you know the rules." They began walking back and we followed. But something started feeling not right.

"Dude," Tyler whispered at me, "I don't like this. I think they're on to us."

I looked back. The door we'd come in was about 70 yards away, and getting farther with every step. Even worse, the room was barren; there were no objects to hide behind. If we had to make a break for it we'd be sitting ducks. These people were trained to kill the most protected individuals on earth. Picking us off would be like a pleasant diversion.

We reached the rest of the group and the man introduced us. "These are new trainees, just joining us for the first time. Your names again are...."

"I'm Dirk Muncie."

"I'm Marcus Jorgenson."

"Didn't you say your name was Tyler?" the man asked.

"Yeah, that's my middle name. My mom named me Marcus, but I can't stand that name."

"So what should we call you?"

"I like 'Thor.'"

"Thor?"

"Hammer of the gods, dude," Tyler said, and then broke into his ninja dance. "See, I got the moves already!"

"He's kidding," I interjected. "Marcus is fine for him."

"Well, it's nice to have both of you with us," the man said, totally indifferent to Tyler's antics. "We have a very special day planned today. One of our graduates will be working a highly critical event soon, and so we're going to be reviewing how he got to where he is."

The other man leaned toward the first and said, "I believe there was a termination exercise planned for today."

"Yes, I realize our newest trainees have arrived, but there's been a last minute change in the schedule. It just came down; today we're going to be singing the praises of and wishing good luck to our very own Todd Manderville."

Anticipating an unwanted reaction, I grabbed Tyler's arm.

"Everyone have a seat," the first man said. We all sat on the floor, and he continued. "Todd Manderville first came to us three years ago. He was a skinny kid, undisciplined and unformed. But he went through the program here and mined the depths of his full potential. Today, Todd's ready to achieve the level of the most honored, right up there with Lee and Sirhan."

"Aw!" Tyler gasped, and I grabbed his arm again.

"Yes, that is amazing," the man said. "And it just goes to show how dedication and hard work can pay off."

"Excuse me," I said. "Will Todd actually be pulling the trigger in this mission or will he just be a decoy?"

"Oh, he's the one who's going to do the job. We have complete confidence in his marksmanship and fortitude."

"What if the target escapes or is only wounded?"

"What good questions you ask. Your mind is already in the

game. All I can say is 'you'll see.' Todd will complete his mission successfully, and by our next meeting we'll have a new president— one who knows how to play by the rules."

"What if something happens to Todd? Is there someone else who can step in and do the job?"

"No. Todd is the one who's been trained for it. If he can't do it, then the project will have to be postponed indefinitely. But nothing's going to happen to Todd. He'll be ready to go."

Tyler and I looked at each other. "I have to go to the bathroom," he said.

"We have breaks scheduled every half hour. Do you think you can wait?"

"No, dude," Tyler said, crossing his legs and squirming. "I gotta get a subscription for Flomax. It's bad. I'm about to make a puddle right here."

"Well, if you have to go that bad. There's a restroom off of the classroom you went through when you came here."

"Oh, thanks, dude. You're a life saver." Tyler got up and walked briskly toward the exit. I got up and followed.

"Excuse me, Dirk," said the first man.

I turned around slowly.

"Do you also have to use the restroom?"

"Actually, yes I do. I thought as long as he was going, I assumed everyone could take a break."

The man paused. "Yes, that's fine," he said, and I turned to go. "But just a minute, Hirk." I stopped again without turning. "Please leave the camera with us."

I gingerly reached into my pocket, removed the camera, laid it on the ground, and continued walking. "Dude," Tyler said. "He just called you Hank. He knows who you are."

I wasn't sure what I heard, but was willing to believe the

worst by now. Then I thought I heard a metallic click come from behind. Our pace quickened the closer we got to the exit, so that we were practically running by the time we reached the door. Inside the classroom, we barreled through so fast we knocked over a desk. I got to the hallway door first, but Tyler jumped in front and grabbed the knob. We squeezed through together and sprinted down the hallway. Coming to the stairs, we tripped a couple times on the way up, banged ourselves into the metal door at the top, and threw it open. Surprised that none of the doors so far had been locked, we had just one more to go before we were back in the outside world. I hesitated for a split second, looked at Tyler, and tried the knob. It opened and we were out. We climbed back through the ditch and tree line, and ran past the quarry buildings. As we passed the last one and headed up the road to Tyler's car, I heard Jim yell out, "Y'all come back now, ya hear?"

We climbed into Tyler's car. I was so out of breath my lungs were burning. Tyler threw in a song called Rebirth of Tragedy by a band called Vision of Disorder, and he peeled out down Piney Meetinghouse Road. I didn't feel even mildly safe until we were a mile onto I-270.

29

As we rode up Georgia Ave toward Wheaton I told Tyler he should stay at his parents' house and not come out until after everything had gone down. He was absolutely not to tag along with me or do any investigating on his own. I didn't want to have to explain it to his father if anything happened to him.

I also thought about Amber. She was to have done the deed on Todd the previous day. But antifreeze took 24 hours to complete its process on the human body. If she'd done it when she said, right now Todd would likely still be alive, but extremely ill. I felt sick myself at the thought that I knew someone had been poisoned and was in the process of dying, but not dead yet. And yet I was sitting there allowing it to happen. I had to remind myself of who Todd was.

I wanted to contact Amber and find out if everything was going as planned. So I scrawled a note on a piece of paper asking her to call me from a pay phone at her first opportunity. Then I told Tyler to drive over to her place.

"This is what I want you to do," I said. "Run up to her front door, stick this in the screen door, ring the bell, then run back here, and we take off." I didn't want to approach Amber myself since Turdington would be looking for me. He also knew Tyler, but I didn't think he thought Tyler was involved. However, I still didn't want Tyler spending too much time at Amber's house because not only were there still a number of nefarious characters out there other than Turdington, if something horrific was in the process of occurring inside Amber's house vis-à-vis Todd, I didn't want Tyler to be exposed to it.

We got to Amber's house and I ducked down near the floor of the car. Tyler ran up and ran back, and we sped away. Mission accomplished. When we got to my bus stop, Tyler said, "Dude, before you go, I gotta play one song for you."

"No, Tyler. That's okay. Really."

"I might never see you again, Hank. Just give it a listen." He put a CD in the player. The band was Snapcase and the song was called "Caboose." The usual heavy, frenetic instrumentation was followed by screamed lyrics. When it was over, Tyler said, "I hope that meant something to you, dude."

"Tyler, I couldn't understand a word he was saying."

He spoke out a few of the lyrics. "'Do you know yourself? Do you know the others? Can you pull the weight that rides on another's shoulders?' It's a song about getting to who you really are deep down and freeing yourself to be a leader and do great things."

"Well, I appreciate the sentiment. Now please stay home until after Monday."

I waited for the bus, eager to hear from Amber. I couldn't stand the thought of not knowing whether Todd was alive or dead, or writhing in agony as I sat there. I needed closure. I got back to Julia's house and waited some more. As the afternoon went into evening, the sun set and I still hadn't heard anything. Then my phone rang. It was Amber. I didn't want to discuss details over the phone, so I gave her directions to Julia's house and asked her to make sure she wasn't followed. About a half hour later I heard a car pull up outside. Seeing Amber get out, I opened the door and hustled her in.

I went to hug her, but barely got any reciprocation. "Are you okay?" I asked.

"Yeah, fine," she said, without looking me in the eye.

"Come, sit down." I went and got her some of Julia's herbal tea. Sitting next to her on the couch, I asked, "Is it all done?"

She nodded her head.

"Do you want to talk about what happened?"

"No," she said, and rested her head on my shoulder.

"It's alright. You did the right thing," I said, and kissed her on the forehead. We sat in silence for a minute before I decided to try to get her mind off what had just happened at her house. "Do you still want to give me a blowjob on the swings?"

She smiled a little for the first time and reached down to my groin. She rubbed and caressed the area, but—though I was certainly getting aroused—Amber's heart didn't seem to be in it. She was just going through the motions. We unbuttoned and unzipped my pants, exposing my erect penis. But Amber didn't use her mouth, she only stroked with her hand, again without any real feeling or conviction. Still, I was getting more and more excited, and I was just about to orgasm, when suddenly the door flew open. I jerked my head up and standing there in the doorway, staring at me and Amber, were Julia and her mother Peggy.

"Hank!" Julia yelled.

"Oh... My... God!" declared Peggy.

"Julia!" I exclaimed, stuffing my penis back in my pants. "When did you get out? I mean, holy shit. How did you escape?"

"What have you been doing here in my house?" Julia asked, as Amber got up, said "Excuse me," and went out the door.

"Is this what you've been doing," yelled Peggy, "while I've been out looking for my kidnapped daughter? Who I thought was supposed to be your friend? Who you said you wouldn't rest until you found her?"

"Thanks a lot, Hank," Julia added.

"Do you know what I had to go through to get Julia back?" said Peggy.

"I hope you didn't make a mess on that sofa," said Julia.

"I got arrested," said Peggy. "And when I called you at all three of your phone numbers and left message after message, you never called back. You could care less if I'm rotting in jail. All you care about is your sick perversions and using my daughter's house for orgies after she's been kidnapped. Oh, my God. I can't believe you."

"It's not what it looks?" I said, questioning if that was the right thing to say.

"It's exactly what it looks," declared Peggy. "And thank you for permanently planting an image of your penis in my brain. I think I'm going to be sick!"

"Hank, you should be more considerate of my mom. She did amazing things to get me back."

"I had to talk to everybody," said Peggy. "Nobody was doing anything. I said 'My daughter's been kidnapped! What are you people doing? Have you heard about rape? Have you heard about dismemberment? While you're sitting there eating donuts, you might as well start dragging Chesapeake Bay!' I had to go to the top to get anybody to listen. I talked to the Prince George's County sheriff, Prince George's chief of police, Montgomery County sheriff, Montgomery chief of police, District of Columbia chief of police, the superintendent of the Maryland State Police, the director of the FBI, and senator Joe Lieberman!"

"You spoke to Joe Lieberman?"

"Yes, I spoke to Joe Lieberman. What were you doing while I was hitting my head against a wall to get in to see Joe Lieberman? Going to massage parlors?"

"Tell him how you got arrested," said Julia.

"Oh, don't get me started. I went to the White House to talk to Obama about all this because nobody seemed to care about doing their job...."

"Wait a minute, excuse me," I said. "Julia, did they let you go voluntarily? Are they going to be looking for you?"

"If they know what's good for them," said Peggy, "they won't come after her."

"The police are supposed to have extra patrols," said Julia, "to make sure everything's okay."

"So the police and the kidnappers could be coming to this house," I said. "I've got to go."

"Hank, you don't want to hear what happened?" asked Julia. "Wait, I want to hear about you and that floozy."

I got myself together and headed for the door.

"Oh, so now he's running away again," said Peggy. "You ran away from a relationship with my daughter; you run away when she's kidnapped and needs your help; and now you run away again. When are you going to grow up, Hank!?" Peggy's voice faded as I left the house.

30

The police and the assassins were looking for me, and now that Todd was dead Special Agent Turdington was certain to ramp up the dragnet for me as well. Even if he wasn't FBI, the real FBI was sure to now take an interest. I wasn't going to hang around. I wanted to get completely out of the area.

At this point I was paranoid being anywhere in the DC region. And I needed time to think. Todd's death may have stopped the plotters for now, but they were still out there. I had to find someone in a position of authority whom I could trust with all the information I now knew. But then my perceived involvement in the deaths of Greg Tousand and Todd Manderville might make it difficult for such an authority to trust me. I had to get away and clear my head.

I thought of my clients up in Waterloo, Norbert and Phyllis Graham. They were in their early 50s; their kids were grown up and they had adequate life insurance, but they needed their retirement planning tweaked. So I'd rolled over an IRA for them and consolidated their other investments under the NALIC umbrella, moving the bulk—based on their ages—out of risky high-yield equity funds into various bond instruments and blue-chip stocks. They had a nice 60/40 bond to equity mix when I was done that I planned to adjust more toward the fixed-income side as they approached and entered retirement. They were grateful for my work, and they were some of the nicest clients I'd ever had. I felt they might be open to helping out.

Waterloo was 14 miles up the road from Calverton—20 miles out of DC. It was perfect. I just needed a ride since the bus didn't go all the way up there. I got on it anyway so I could get out of the area, and I called Norbert. Even though it was after 9:00pm, he agreed without question to come pick me up. He met me at Burtonsville Crossing, the bus route's terminus, and before long we were at the Graham home on Hicks Road in Waterloo.

Norbert was employed at the Little Patuxent Water Reclamation Plant and Phyllis worked part time at a middle-school cafeteria. They were stable, church-going people far removed from the seemingly endless rat race and depths of self interest that plagued the populace closer to DC.

Their house smelled of home-cooked meals and fresh-out-of-the-dryer linen. Pictures of their kids wearing mortar boards, and one son in his Marine uniform, adorned end tables along with several Hummel figurines. I felt I was six years old again spending an eagerly anticipated weekend with my grandparents.

We had a roast beef dinner, with apple pie for dessert. The Grahams didn't pry much, but during dinner Phyllis did gently ask why I had to get out of my area. I suggested I was having trouble with my significant other—a claim not wholly untrue—and that the Grahams were the nicest folks I knew. That night I slept in the guest room, which had been their son's bedroom when he was home. It was quiet and deeply comfortable.

The next morning I was offered a breakfast of over-easy

eggs, bacon, and Cap'n Crunch cereal. Then we went to church. The Grahams belonged to the Wesley Chapel United Methodist Church. The pastor's sermon that day had a Memorial Day theme and he lauded the church's "Adopt-a-Platoon" program. They had quite a good choir, and I sang along to the hymns. Then we stayed for fellowship and Sunday school.

The adult Sunday-school class was essentially a Bible study group; a passage was read and then discussed around the table. The passage for the day was, "Now Israel loved Joseph more than any other of his children, because he was the son of his old age; and he had made him a long robe with sleeves. But when his brothers saw that their father loved him more than all his brothers, they hated him, and could not speak peaceably to him."

"Excuse me," I said. "Is that the New Revised Standard Version?"

"Yes, it is," came the reply.

"Thank you," I said, and kept my mouth shut for the rest of the class.

Afterward, we went back to the Grahams where we had a lunch of bologna sandwiches on white bread. Then Norbert and I went out to do some yard work. I trimmed hedges while Norbert mowed. As I worked, it came over me that I had to get back to DC. My time with the Grahams had been positively bucolic, but I wanted to go to Arlington Cemetery.

Even though the plot—based on what I'd heard at the training camp—would not go forward without Todd, I wanted to be there anyway. I wanted to be there to see President Obama successfully survive the ceremony, and also be there in case the plotters had come up with a contingency. I knew it would be a huge risk with so many people who wished me ill on the lookout, but I had an overwhelming desire to do it. I hadn't come this far just to watch the culmination of my last two months' blood, sweat, and tears on somebody's television.

I mentioned the idea to the Grahams, and Norbert initially resisted, saying he was planning on watching the final round of the Byron Nelson golf tournament. But then he thought how he hadn't been to Arlington during Memorial weekend for quite some time, and warmed up to the idea. I asked one last favor before we piled into the Grahams' car: Could I borrow one of Norbert's outfits? I picked a pair of white shorts, a Hawaiian shirt, a golf hat, a pair of sunglasses, and we were off.

We got to Arlington around 5:00pm, and walked along the pathways looking at the green seas filled with thousands of uniformly spaced identical white headstones. Each stone had a little American flag stuck in ground in front of it. This was "flags in" Norbert explained, a Memorial weekend tradition. A quarter million little flags waved in front of an equal number of stones throughout the cemetery.

Norbert showed me the headstone of his uncle, an Army Air Corps pilot who was killed in World War II. We went up to John F. Kennedy's gravesite. The eternal flame bent in the wind, but remained undiminished. We went over to Robert Kennedy's grave, marked by a small white cross at the base of the hill in front of Robert E. Lee's former home. We visited the Civil War Unknowns Monument and the old Custis-Lee Mansion, now called Arlington House, where Lee lived before agreeing to lead the Army of Northern Virginia in the Civil War. The North had promptly taken over the land and turned his front yard into a Union burial ground.

I wanted to go to the Tomb of the Unknowns, where the sentinels walked and where the wreath-laying ceremony was to take place the following day. But it was getting close to 7:00pm, closing time for the cemetery, and the Grahams were getting fatigued. I said I thought I'd stay and look around a bit more, and then take the Metro back home. I thanked them for their hospitality, saying I'd like to visit again soon. And I meant it.

31

After bidding the Grahams farewell, I headed in the direction of the Tomb of the Unknowns. But instead of going there, I surveyed the landscape and found the largest tree among a group of trees far off the roadway. I went and, sitting down behind it, waited until dark.

By 9:00pm it was getting dark, and I moved to an area where I could watch the sentinels from a distance as they walked. They only changed once every hour at night, and I watched the same guard walk methodically to and fro without the slightest variation for almost the full hour. Then the change occurred. I couldn't see the details from where I was, but the next guard eventually began his walk and was as exact and methodical as the previous guard had been. I thought how this went on exactly the same way 24 hours a day, 365 days a year, with slight variations only during ceremonies such as the wreath laying. But with all its exactitude, no one was expecting the variation in the ritual that certain people had planned for the following day, a variation that now apparently would not take place.

I went back to my tree and settled in for the night. The low temperature was supposed to be in the mid 50s, so with my shorts and Hawaiian shirt, I'd have to tuck my body in as much as possible to conserve warmth. Soon I found myself asleep among the headstones.

I woke up around 6:45 the next morning. The cemetery was already illuminated by brilliant sunshine, and I was glad I hadn't been discovered. The place didn't open to the public until 8:00am, so I had to stay vigilant until then. I had to urinate and couldn't hold it. So, staying behind my tree, I sent the stream out as far as possible so as not to sully my area. The disrespect inherent in taking a giant leak among the headstones at Arlington National Cemetery did cross my mind. But I rationalized by convincing myself I was there to protect the life of the commander-in-chief, which would be impossible if I were to go down to the visitors center an hour before the cemetery opened to use the rest room. I would promptly be detained as a trespasser and that would be that.

I waited by my tree for another hour and a half. I watched the wind rustle through the leaves in the trees around my area, watched birds come and go, watched the little "flags in" flags anticipate a gust of wind on the other side of the section before it reached me. By 8:15 I decided it was safe to reenter the normal flow of things at the cemetery. I brushed myself off and went back to the walkway.

Memorial Day was perhaps the busiest day of the year at Arlington, so there were already people coming in and walking around. I'd blend in very nicely. I didn't go back to the visitors center for food or facilities in case someone noticed I hadn't come through there that morning. Instead, I went up toward the Tomb and the Memorial Amphitheater. On the way I noticed a larger, more elaborate gravestone than the standard-issue small white ones. Upon closer examination, I saw it was for heavyweight boxing champ Joe Louis. Right next to his was a standard stone; it was for movie star Lee Marvin. "Ain't that America?" I said, and moved on.

When I got to the vicinity of the Tomb and Amphitheater I came upon a Secret Service checkpoint. Everyone was being screened through metal detectors and searched. I got in with no problem, but thought how futile this effort was when there would be soldiers in there later all armed with rifles. And there would have been one among them with live ammo and malevolent designs, if his money-hungry wife hadn't intervened first.

The wreath-laying ceremony was to take place shortly before 11:00. I got to the steps leading from the Amphitheater to the Tomb a little after 9:00. This was the area from where the general public would be observing the ceremony. I'd gotten there early enough that I found a spot right in front along the railing. Then, for the next hour and a half, I watched the guards.

They moved exactly the same as the last time I'd seen them —fluid, but with intense precision. Their footfalls were so exact that they'd left permanent marks on the paving stones. And along the path where the sentinel on duty did his regular walk, a black mat had been put down so that the tens of thousands of steps taken on those exact same spots every day would not wear holes in the stones. Each sentinel walked 15 steps every 10 seconds, and never wavered from that pace. They took 21 steps in each direction, and paused 21 seconds in the middle of each turn. At every half hour exactly, a sergeant—the relief commander—came out and led the changing of the guard.

Among his first duties was, in an exceptionally official tone, addressing the spectators: "Ladies and gentlemen, may I have your attention please? I am Staff Sergeant Merriweather of the 3rd Infantry Regiment, United States Army, commander of the relief, Tomb of the Unknown Soldier. The ceremony that you are about to witness is the changing of the guard. In keeping with the dignity of this ceremony it is requested that everyone remain silent and standing. Thank you." His next major task was to inspect the incoming sentinel. The sergeant spent nearly two minutes painstakingly inspecting the soldier's rifle alone, before turning to his uniform.

I saw three guard changes before the wreath-laying ceremony. The first two followed the same patterns, as did the third. But there was something different with the third change. I was suddenly struck with the feeling I was seeing familiar faces. The sergeant who came out for this change was not the same as in the previous changes. He stood right in front of me, and even though he wore sunglasses I recognized him as the sergeant from Tyler's video. He began his speech, "Ladies and gentlemen, may I have your attention please? I am Sergeant Teetsel...."

Now I had a name to go with the face. He went and did the inspection on the new guard, very carefully checking his rifle and giving it back. And when the new guard walked to the center, I recognized him too. I was surprised to see it was Private Peter Huguenot. He'd told me at the airport he would be away on leave until after Memorial Day. But now here he was. Perhaps, I thought, Todd's absence had made it necessary to call him back early.

Private Huguenot began his walk and Sergeant Teetsel went back to the guard quarters. Shortly thereafter the Army band, which had been playing inside the Amphitheater, came out to the Tomb area so they could be in place to play the national anthem upon the president's arrival. Then contingents of honor guards from each branch of the service marched up the steps from the other side of the Tomb, taking positions on each side of it. The Coast Guard, Army, Navy, Marines, and Air Force all stood at attention facing the spectators. By this time, Private Huguenot had stopped walking and was standing at attention off to the side.

Excitement began building in the crowd, and I could hear several conversations going on. Most of them were benign comments about the ceremony, but a few were not so pleasant. One man in particular was not a fan of Barack Obama, saying he didn't know why he would even come to do the wreath laying because "he clearly hates our way of life."

Then several dignitaries came up the walkway. The secretary of defense, first lady, and others lined up in front of the railing where I stood. A few other people came along—photographers, Secret Service agents. Then President Obama walked onto the scene with the commanding general of the U.S. Army military district of Washington, and took a position in front of the black mat.

My line of vision went past Obama's head to the front row of the Army's honor guard contingent. And there he was. I was sure of it. I strained my eyes and concentrated. But it was him. Todd Manderville was standing first from the left.

I didn't know what to do. I was flabbergasted. But I had to think fast. There was President Obama and there was Todd Manderville standing no more than 12 yards away from him holding an M-14 rifle. Not to mention, I was directly in his line of fire.

A command was shouted: "Present... arms!" The soldiers all lifted their rifles from their sides to a high vertical position. One more move and Todd would have an easy shot. The commanding general saluted and President Obama put his hand on his heart as the band started into the Star Spangled Banner.

I thought of jumping the rail and disrupting the proceedings. But that would only delay things for a while. I'd be arrested, and they'd regroup and continue. I decided I had to make my case to the nearest Secret Service agent, and just hope he was one of the good guys.

"Excuse me," I said, waving to the agent looking into the crowd nearby. He noticed me, said something into his sleeve, and came over.

"Sir, what is this about?" he said as the band played on.

"There's a soldier over there with a loaded rifle who's going to shoot President Obama." I looked over at Todd who was standing rock still with his rifle at present arms.

"Sir, no there isn't," the agent said as he continued scanning the crowd. "Please remain calm and be quiet." He started walking away. The band entered the final strains of the anthem. The cymbals crashed once.

"Yes, there is," I said, raising my voice enough to attract the attention of another Secret Service agent. "And I won't be quiet!" Someone in the crowd shushed me; the first agent again said something into his sleeve. The other agent held his position as the first agent started back toward me. Then the band hit the final cymbal crash and last note of the tune.

"A soldier named Todd Manderville," I told him, "in the front row over there is going to shoot the president."

"Listen to me," the agent said as more calls for quiet cascaded from the crowd. "We've got the situation completely under control."

"No, you don't!" I yelled, and lifted my leg over the railing.

At that point, a command went out to the soldiers: "Order... arms!" And in the space of one second, all hell broke loose.

Not lowering his rifle to order arms, instead Private Huguenot leveled it and pointed it directly at President Obama. Todd Manderville also did not lower his rifle. He leveled it at Private Huguenot and fired. Instantly after Todd's shot, Private Huguenot's rifle also discharged. Huguenot then crumpled to the ground as pandemonium ensued. Spectators screamed and stampeded in a panic up the steps toward the Amphitheater. Around 10 Secret Service agents, most seemingly coming from nowhere, converged on the scene as dozens of soldiers, sailors, air men, and marines scrambled around, mostly in the areas where Todd and Huguenot had stood. Commanders barked orders, but general mayhem continued. Then more shots were fired.

Secret Service, cemetery security, and Army personnel raced back and forth as two large scrums of military men and Secret Service agents formed around Todd and Huguenot. More shouting ensued; commanders again tried to reestablish order. Meanwhile, the president was gone.

I'd been ducking and keeping an eye on the people with the guns, and when I looked back I no longer saw President Obama. The first lady and other dignitaries had also left. But not the secretary of defense. He was lying on his side in a fetal position as two cemetery security officers leaned over him.

After a couple of minutes some semblance of control began returning to the area. Military commanders got their men back in formation, and medical personnel began arriving on the scene. I could see EMTs with the secretary of defense and with Private Huguenot. There was also one with Todd, who lay on the ground motionless. But he wasn't there long. Two Secret Service agents— including the one I'd been speaking to—along with two soldiers picked up Todd's limp body and hustled it around the corner of the building toward the guard quarters. At that point, cemetery security told the few remaining spectators, including me, to leave the area.

I tried to hang around and see whatever I could, but security officials at every turn were ushering people toward the cemetery exit. So, along with hundreds of others, I simply walked out the main entrance. I got on the Metro and rode the Blue Line out of there.

32

Feeling it advisable to get one more motel room, I got off the train in College Park and got set up. I ordered Chinese food—I hadn't eaten since the Grahams' bologna sandwiches the previous day. Then, just as millions of other people were doing at that moment throughout the country and around the world, I watched what had happened on television.

It turned out President Obama was safe and uninjured. The bullet meant for him had missed and instead struck the secretary of defense, who was in the hospital in serious but stable condition. The man who had done the shooting was Peter Douglas Huguenot, a private in the U.S. Army. He was also in the hospital, in critical condition, having been shot through the lungs. The man who shot him was being hailed as a hero. He was Corporal Todd Manderville, also of the U.S. Army. Corporal Manderville, unfortunately, had been killed in the melee that followed the shooting, apparently by an errant Secret Service bullet.

Over the next 12 hours, I ordered more Chinese food and watched the cable news networks fall all over themselves trying to get scoops on the others. The biggest scoop of all occurred that evening when it came out that more arrests had been made. There seemed to have been a wider conspiracy, and several law enforcement agencies were in the process of detaining other people. The first name to be mentioned was unfamiliar to me: Toby Moss. But when one of the networks obtained a picture, it turned out to be my old buddy pentagram. Checkers, aka, Angelo Gennarelli, came shortly thereafter. They also picked up Sergeant Teetsel, and then the big names began to fall. The authorities had taken into custody Tim Johnson, who was my "host" at the Secret Service, and even Major Brian Warner of the Pentagon. I couldn't believe it. Not only had President Obama survived, but they were actually catching the perpetrators this time. Then the head enchilada came tumbling down. William Bradford was shown being led in handcuffs out of the office building where he ran his noxious weeds empire.

So far there was no mention of me, which was a relief. But of concern was the fact that Susan Underhill—the person who actually shot the person I was accused of shooting—was not mentioned among those who'd been picked up. Then my phone rang around 11:00. It was Amber.

"Hello," I said.

"Hello," she said back.

"How are you doing?"

"Feeling crappy."

I had lots of questions, but didn't quite know how to make the approach. "What's bothering you the most?" I ended up saying.

"Everything," she said.

"Is there something I can do?"

"No, Hank. I just wanted to call to say goodbye."

"Goodbye? What's going on? Are you okay?"

"Yeah, I'm okay. I mean I'm not going to kill myself, if that's what you mean."

This was a mood I'd never seen in Amber before. And I wasn't sure which of the recent events might have triggered it. It could have been anything, including the possibility that she was really one of the bad guys all along, and had tried to kill Todd and failed before he'd completed his mission. I had to find out. "Are you happy that Todd is being called a hero?"

"Yeah, I guess."

"Okay, Amber. I have to know. What's really bothering you?"

"Todd and I," she told me. "We'd fallen back in love." Amber must have sensed my speechlessness and she continued. "He started taking me out on dates again. He became obsessed with that game you showed us. Duckpins. It's harder than regular bowling and Todd took it as a challenge. He always wanted to be the best in the most difficult things. But he wanted to include me too. We were drifting apart before that. I didn't feel a connection with him at all anymore. But he was really excited about duckpins and he wanted me to be part of it. We talked a lot while we were there. And on that day. You know, the day I told you I was going to.... Well, normally he would come home from the base and go to the basement to do his workout and I wouldn't see him. This time he said he'd rather spend the time with me and we went bowling. And while we were there, he got down on his knee and proposed to me all over again. He told me he loved me and wanted to make a fresh start. He was really sincere and meant it. I knew I couldn't go through with the plan anymore. And I knew I couldn't see you anymore. I came to that house the other night to see you one last time and say goodbye."

"Duckpins," I said. "Who would have thought?"

"And now I won't see him anymore," she said and started to cry.

"It's okay, Amber," I said. "Do you have anyone you can talk to?"

"My best friend is downstairs and my mom's coming in from Ohio."

"Good," I said. "You know, if you ever want to hang out some time...."

"I just need time to think right now. Maybe some other time."

"I understand, Amber. If there's anything I can do, let me know."

"Thank you, Hank. Goodbye."

"Bye." I hung up the phone. "Well, I'll be," I said to myself.

I stayed in my motel room the next day watching more news. Then my worst fear was realized. My name was mentioned on TV in connection with the Tousand murder. But then a reprieve. At a news conference an FBI spokesman explained that Tousand was suspected to have been killed on orders from William Bradford. "But there is a witness to the murder who we would very much like to speak with. DC police received an anonymous tip a few days ago that Henry A. Stafford of Beltsville, Maryland, was standing near Mr. Tousand when Mr. Tousand was shot."

"I'll bet it was an anonymous tip," I said.

"I'd like to make it clear," the spokesman continued, "Mr. Stafford is not a suspect. We believe he had nothing to do with the crime. But he is a material witness and we would like to speak with him."

That sounded good to me. And with Bradford, Johnson, pentagram, and checkers wrapped up I thought I could finally stop spending all this money on motel rooms and TracFones. Being chased by assassins and the police was a problem, but the negative cash flow in my bank account was starting to give me an ulcer.

33

I went to FBI headquarters—from where I'd been chased after Tousand's murder—and had my interview. Oddly, it was very short. They only asked a few questions about what I'd seen and who I saw do it. Even though Susan Underhill was still at large, they seemed more interested in clearing me than in pursuing her.

So that was that. I went back to my home for the first time in weeks. And, as I suspected, it had been trashed. I spent the better part of the next two days getting it back in shape. I also went to the office, where Rich Fox was very forgiving about the explosion that had made almost a third of the NALIC floor space uninhabitable. "You can have a bigger office for now," he said. "And if you make Million Dollar Round Table this year you can keep it. But I'm leaving your old office as is, and if you don't make MDRT, you're going back into it next year."

Rich enjoyed creating little incentives for his agents. In any event, I had a lot of catching up to do. I had to get back to building my book of business in a serious way, and I began working on how I could parlay my experiences with the assassins into marketable selling points when prospecting and closing with clients.

That Sunday I watched "This Week with George Stephanopoulos," and the assassination attempt was the big topic of discussion. George Will mentioned he believed he'd had a brush with one of the perpetrators himself. "This man, this insurance salesman, who was subsequently cleared by the FBI, was found to have broken into my home. At the time, being the good, noble, live-and-let-live fellow that I am, I declined to press charges. I'm now regretting my decision because it appears he's more involved in all this than the federal government is letting on. Records show that he met with Timothy Johnson, the Secret Service man who was arrested; he had a meeting with Peter Douglas Huguenot in the weeks prior to the attempt on President Obama's life; he met with Major Warner at the Pentagon; he was there when this Tousand fellow was murdered; in the days before the assassination attempt he was seen going into the Committee for Noxious Weeds, the same agency led by one William Bradford; and he was at the Tomb of the Unknown Soldier when the attempt on President Obama was made. But here's the kicker. He was the agent who sold the life insurance policy on Todd's life to the Mandervilles. Now if all of that doesn't raise at least a few eyebrows down at the Department of Justice, then I don't know what would."

"Are you suggesting," George Stephanopoulos asked, "that the federal government is covering something up?"

"Not at all. I'm suggesting that, par for the course, the federal government is mishandling a task that we the people have entrusted to it. I'm suggesting that the more we rely on government to provide us with answers and solutions, the longer we will have to wait before any useful answers and solutions are actually forthcoming."

I had to admit, it looked a little funny. But I figured as long as George Will was more upset with the government than he was with me, I'd be alright.

A couple of weeks passed and I was getting back into the swing of my normal life. Then one night I was riding the Green Line back from a late evening appointment. There were two people in the car, myself and a woman who was sitting down at the other end. The doors closed on the Shaw-Howard University station and we were still the only people in the car. But a few seconds later I heard a loud, rumbling cough. I looked up to see Robert Livingstone sitting down next to me.

"Good evening, Mr. Stafford," he said in a smoker's voice times 10.

"Where did you come from?"

"You know where I come from," he said. "You've seen my digs. Don't play coy with me."

"No, I mean...."

"I know what you mean. Lighten up." He cleared his throat. "So how's life?"

"Getting back to normal, thanks. But I see some of your friends got arrested."

"God, don't say that. Those people weren't my friends."

"I thought you were all in the same business together."

"Maybe so. But this business does not lend itself to fraternization. So a few got caught. Business is still as strong as ever."

"It is?"

"Of course. They picked up seven people and stopped there. This is a contingency we've had planned for decades. What's surprising is it never happened sooner."

"So nothing changes?"

"Bigs come and Bigs go. But the church goes on, my dear."

"Why aren't they looking for Susan Underhill?"

"The church goes on."

"And the training site, and the trainers, the trainees, all of the operatives posted around the country?"

Livingstone shrugged his shoulders.

"And when they said at the training camp that Todd was...."

"Disinformation for your benefit."

"Uh huh. And if the police went there they would find...."

"Nothing."

"Of course."

"Mais oui."

"So who's going to be the new Mr. Big?"

"You're looking at him."

"I don't know whether to congratulate you or not."

"Not."

"You don't know that I know your real name."

"Tell me my real name; I'd love to hear it."

"Robert Livingstone."

"No, that's not my real name." He let out a booming cough. "But I applaud your investigation skills."

"What about Artemus Schreckengost?"

"I could tell you about Artemus Schreckengost."

"But you'd have to kill me?"

"No, you'd have to join us."

"Is that what you're doing? Are you trying to recruit me?"

"We're always looking for a few good men, so to speak."

"I'm sorry, I already have a job."

"It doesn't hurt to ask. You understand."

I did understand. My entire career was built on that simple foundation. "Yeah," I said, "I'm afraid I do."

"Take Todd Manderville, for example. He was a good man. Too good to waste."

"What do you mean?"

Livingstone smiled at me. "Your friends at the FBI, Secret Service, and the Army played this one much better than they ever have in the past. They learned a little something after all. They play their hand, we play ours. This time they had one better card than we did."

I looked blank.

"You still don't get it? Todd Manderville isn't dead. His death was faked by the government. He's too valuable to be killed, but what he did was too public to maintain his cover. His death was faked, his identity changed, and now he's in training for his next mission."

"How do you know all this?"

"Hank, please. We still have a card or two up our own sleeve."

"But, I don't know if you know this...."

"That you're a beneficiary on his life insurance policy?"

"Why did I even doubt?"

"Don't worry about that. You'll find the government is going to do right by you."

Robert Livingstone was one of the nicest people I'd met during this whole episode, but I couldn't help remembering what it was he did for a living. "I don't know," I said. "I just have a problem with this business you're in. The president lived this time. But what about the next time? How do you know I won't go to the FBI and tell them about you?"

"Please, Hank. Feel free to go to the feds and tell them anything you want. I don't mind about that. And about this other thing. I told you I would not have set the training to a degree where it would take out this president. I can't vouch for future Bigs, but as long as I'm around I can guarantee a subtler approach. A White House intern sex scandal is much more my style."

"Are you saying Monica Lewinsky was...."

"Mm hmm."

"Wow."

"Hank, it's been a real pleasure." Livingstone stood up. "I wish you only the best in all your endeavors."

"I wish I could say the same for you."

"That hurt."

"Good luck to you."

He bowed, turned, let out a huge cough, and walked to the middle of the car. We were about a minute from the Fort Totten stop. I looked out the window for a few seconds, and when I turned back, Livingstone was gone.

It turned out George Will wasn't the only one who thought my involvement with the Mandervilles was concerning. Amber had filed her death benefit claim with NALIC, and NALIC had come back saying they weren't going to pay. They wanted to do an investigation first because not only had Todd died under unusual circumstances so soon after the policy was issued, but the agent who sold it was named as a beneficiary. Plus this agent had been behaving in an odd manner the last few weeks.

It was looking like it was going to be a tough fight, but Robert Livingstone was right. Unsolicited by me, NALIC received letters from the FBI, Secret Service, and U.S. Army. The letters assured NALIC Amber and I were completely innocent of everything. They were glowing reports that painted me almost as a saint. And they weren't just signed by middle-management types. The commanding general of the U.S. Army military district of

Washington, who'd been with President Obama when the shooting occurred, signed the one from the Army. The Secret Service assistant director for protective operations signed theirs. And no less than the director of the FBI himself signed the one from the bureau.

NALIC had no choice. They approved the payment. Amber would get her $4 million and I would get my $1 million, all tax free. I was feeling pretty good when I heard the news. But that night, as I walked up to my front door, I heard someone yell, "Lou Gehrig can eat a steaming pile of shit!"

Turning around, I saw Special Agent Theodore Turdington trudging his way toward me.

"Because you, Henry A. Stafford," he continued, "are the luckiest man on the face of the earth."

"Hello...." I began before being cut off.

"No no no no no. Don't say a word. I don't think my delicate constitution can take another thing from you. I want you to listen to me." He took a deep breath. "I just want you to know I don't believe a single word of what my director has been telling the public. I know you, Hank Stafford. I know what you were really doing. And I know once a scumbag always a scumbag."

He pulled a small recorder out of his pocket and pushed a button, never taking his eyes off me the whole time. Out of the recorder came a man's voice. "Go to the middle of the table." There was some moving around and then the man said, "How are you about unprotected sex?" A woman replied, "I'm okay with it. I'm on the pill." Yes, it was me and Amber again. At this rate, I thought, we would be all over the internet in no time. Turdington let the sounds of squeaking and physical exertion play for while, then pushed the stop button.

"You are gonna fuck up one of these days," he said. "And

when you do you better pray you've got enough life insurance on yourself." He began walking backwards. With his eyes fixed on me he said, "I'll be watching you." He turned and walked toward the street, and I went back to my door. Then I heard a loud, banshee wail that echoed against the buildings of the neighborhood, "I'll be watching you!"

Later, I called Julia. She'd been sleeping and my call woke her. We'd spoken since I'd run from her house that night, and she was not upset with me; she knew I'd been trying my best. Her mom, on the other hand, was on her way to hating me for the rest of her life. "Don't worry about her, Hank. My mom shows love in different ways."

"So if she stabbed me with a kitchen knife, it would mean she wanted to marry me?"

"Ha ha. Very funny."

"So I saw Tyler the other day."

"How's he doing?"

"Well, he and a friend of his are starting up a website dedicated to future conspiracies."

"Future conspiracies?"

"Yeah, he said any jackass can put up a site about past events. It takes real skill to come up with content on things that haven't happened yet."

"The entrepreneurial spirit still lives."

"It certainly does. I got him in contact with John Poindexter, who could probably help him out."

"Who's John Poindexter?"

"He's basically a top spook from the Reagan and George W. Bush administrations. He developed a way to predict future assassinations."

"Oh, that John Poindexter. I thought the name sounded familiar."

"Why's that?"

"Because I just heard it on the news. John Poindexter is dead."

"Julia, can I offer you some advice? Don't screw with a man who has post-traumatic stress disorder."

"Sorry. So you want to do anything tomorrow?"

"Well, I just got a million dollars. Let's go see a second-run movie."

"You really know how to spoil a girl."

Epilogue

I got to keep my big office. Rich gave a struggling third-year agent my old bombed-out office with the promise to fix it up once the agent's production reached a certain level. More importantly, I qualified for MDRT with room to spare. The notoriety from the assassination attempt brought me some killer centers of influence, and I almost didn't have time to write all the business that was coming my way. I don't think the little slogan I developed for myself hurt either: "I saved the president's life; let me protect yours!" So I hired a girl to help me process the paperwork. Pleasant, intelligent. If things go well I may ask her to the MDRT Annual Meeting in June.

It'll be the achievement of a lifetime: my first MDRT. The meeting this year is in Salt Lake City, a gathering of the best insurance salespeople in the world. It's sad, in a way, because I know it will be the biggest thrill of my life. A high point that will not be topped. Nothing else could ever compare.